بسم الله الرحمن الرحيم

IN THE NAME OF

ALLAH

THE ALL-COMPASSIONATE, ALL-MERCIFUL

The Prophet Muhammad (ﷺ): The Best of All Husbands

- Title: The Prophet Muhammad (ﷺ)
- The Best of All Husbands
- Author: Dr. Ghazi al-Shammari
- English Edition 1 (2009)
- Translator: Najwa Jaffer
- Layout Design: IIPH, Riyadh, Saudi Arabia
- Filming and Cover Designing: Samo Press Group

The Prophet Muhammad ﷺ The Best of All Husbands

النبي صلى الله عليه وسلم زوجاً

Dr. Ghazi al-Shammari

Translated by

Najwa Jaffer

الدار العالمية للكتاب الإسلامي

INTERNATIONAL ISLAMIC PUBLISHING HOUSE

King Fahd National Library Cataloging-in-Publication Data

Al-Shammari, Ghazi

The Prophet Muhammad: The best of all husbands / Ghazi al-Shammari, translated by Najwa Jaffer .- Riyadh, 2009

...p; ...cm

ISBN Hard Cover: 978-603-501-029-0
ISBN Soft Cover: 978-603-501-027-6

1- Muhammad, Prophet life I- Najwa Jaffer (translator)
II- Title

239 dc 1430/176
1430/107

ISBN Hard Cover: **978-603-501-029-0** Legal Deposit no. **1430/176**
ISBN Soft Cover: **978-603-501-027-6** Legal Deposit no. **1430/107**

International Islamic Publishing House (IIPH)
P.O. Box 55195 Riyadh 11534, Saudi Arabia
Tel: 966 1 4650818 / 4647213 — Fax: 966 1 4633489
E-mail: iiph@iiph.com.sa — iiphsa@gmail.com
www.iiph.com.sa

List of Contents

Arabic honorific symbols used in this book

(سبحانه وتعالى) : *Subḥânahu wa Ta'âla* — "The Exalted"

(صلى الله عليه وسلم) : *Ṣalla-Allâhu 'Alayhi wa Sallam* — "Blessings and peace be upon him"

(عليه السلام) : *'Alayhis-Salâm* — "May peace be upon him"

(رضي الله عنه) : *Raḍia-Allâhu 'Anhu* — "May Allah be pleased with him"

(رضي الله عنها) : *Raḍia-Allâhu 'Anha* — "May Allah be pleased with her"

About the word *Lord*

The word *lord* in English has several related meanings. The original meaning is 'master' or 'ruler', and in this sense it is often used to refer to human beings: 'the lord of the mansion' or 'Lord So-and-so' (in the United Kingdom, for example). The word *Lord* with a capital L is used in the lexicon of Islam to refer to the One and Only God — Allah. In Islam, there is no ambiguity about the meaning of this word. While it is true that one may occasionally use the word *lord* (whether capitalized or not) to refer to a human being, in Islamic discourse the reference of this term is always clear from the context. Whereas for Christians, Hindus and other polytheists, the word *Lord* with a capital L may refer to Allah, to Jesus or to some imagined deity, for Muslims, there can be no plurality of meaning. Allah alone is the Lord, and the Lord is Allah — not Jesus, not Rama, not any other being.

The Editor

Transliteration Chart

Arabic script	Pronunciation	Transliterated as:
أ	short 'a', as in *cat*	a
آ - ى	longer 'a', as in *cab* (not as in *cake*)	â
ب	/b/ as in *bell*, *rubber* and *tab*	b
ت	/t/ as in *tap, mustard* and *sit*	t
ة	takes the sound of the preceding diactrical mark sometimes ending in h (when in pausal form): ah, ih, or ooh; or atu(n), ati(n) or ata(n) when in uninterrupted speech	h or t (when followed by another Arabic word)
ث	/th/ as in *thing*, *maths* and *wealth*	th
ج	/j/ as in *jam*, *ajar* and *age*	j
ح	a 'harsher' sound than the English initial /h/, and may occur medially and in word-final position as well	ḥ
خ	as in *Bach* (in German); may occur initially and medially as well	kh
د	/d/ as in *do*, *muddy* and *red*	d
ذ	as in *this*, *father*, and *with*	dh
ر	/r/ as in *raw*, *art* and *war*; may also be a rolled r, as with Spanish words	r

Arabic script	Pronunciation	Transliterated as:
ز	/z/ as in *zoo*, *easy* and *gaze*	z
س	/s/ as in *so*, *messy* and *grass*	s
ش	as in *ship*, *ashes* and *rush*	sh
ص	no close equivalent in English, but may be approximated by pronouncing it as /sw/ or /s/ farther back in the mouth	ṣ
ض	no close equivalent in English, but may be approximated by pronouncing /d/ farther back in the mouth	ḍ
ط	no close equivalent in English, but may be approximated by pronouncing /t/ farther back in the mouth	ṭ
ظ	no close equivalent in English, but may be approximated by pronouncing 'the' farther back in the mouth	<u>dh</u>
ع	no close equivalent in English: a guttural sound in the back of the throat	'
غ	no close equivalent in English, but may be closely approximated by pronouncing it like the French /r/ in 'rouge'	gh
ف	/f/ as in *fill*, *effort* and *muff*	f

Arabic script	Pronunciation	Transliterated as:
ق	no close equivalent in English, but may be approximated by pronouncing /k/ farther back in the mouth	q
ك	/k/ as in *king*, *buckle* and *tack*	k
ل	/l/ as in *lap*, *halo*; in the word *Allah*, it becomes velarized as in *ball*	l
م	/m/ as in *men*, *simple* and *ram*	m
ن	/n/ as in *net*, *ant* and *can*	n
هـ - ه - ـه	/h/ as in hat; unlike /h/ in English, in Arabic /h/ is pronounced in medial and word-final positions as well	h
و	as in *wet* and *away*	w
و (as a vowel)	long u, as in *boot* and *too*	oo
ي	as in *yet* and *yard*	y
ي (as a vowel)	long e, as in *eat*, *beef* and *see*	ee
ء	glottal stop: may be closely approximated by pronouncing it like 't' in the Cockney English pronunciation of *butter*: *bu'er*, or the stop sound in *uh - oh!*	' (Omitted in initial position)

Diphthongs:

Arabic script	Pronunciation	Transliterated as:
أَو ، و	Long o, as in *owe*, *boat* and *go*	au, aw, ow
أَي ، يَ	Long 'a', as in *able*, *rain* and *say*	ay, ai, ei

Diacritical marks (*tashkeel*):

Name of mark	Pronunciation	Transliterated as:
ـَ fatḥah	very short 'a' or schwa (unstressed vowel)	a
ـِ kasrah	shorter version of ee or schwa (unstressed vowel)	i
ـُ Dammah	shorter version of oo	u
ـّ shaddah	a doubled consonant is stressed in the word, and the length of the sound is also doubled	Double letter
ـْ sukoon	no vowel sound between consonants or at the end of a word	Absence of vowel

THE PROPHET MUHAMMAD(ﷺ): THE BEST OF ALL HUSBANDS

Publisher's Note

All praise and thanks belong to Allah alone, the Almighty, the All-Merciful. Blessings and peace be upon Prophet Muhammad — the last Messenger, his family, his Companions, and all those who follow his example until the end of time.

This book highlights the role played by Prophet Muhammad (ﷺ) within his household and especially as a husband. The author focuses on individual — and beautiful — aspects of his excellent way of dealing with his wives, such as the Prophet's gentleness with them, the way he relaxed and had fun with them and his fairness in dealing with them. And that is what makes this book so special and so appealing.

We hope that this small book shall serve to remind husbands and wives about the blessing of marriage, and to encourage those who are not married to strive to complete their religion in the most honourable way. *Inshâ' Allah*, this reminder will help us all to cherish our families and attain rewards through treating them well.

May Allah accept the efforts of all those who contributed to the production of this book, *Âmeen.*

Muhammad ibn 'Abdul-Muhsin Al-Tuwaijri
Managing Director
International Islamic Publishing House
Riyadh, Saudi Arabia

Translator's Foreword

Looking at recent works in the Muslim world written on marriage and relationships, it seems that there is a tendency to focus on the role of women in making a marriage successful, while ignoring the responsibilities of their male counterparts.

Whilst reading and translating this work, it was refreshing to see how the author ventured to sound a slightly different note, by reminding men, in his most gentle and kind approach, that we have the example of the best husband in our Prophet (ﷺ), and the men of our societies have a lot to learn from his eminent example. Yet, he does not place the entire responsibility of achieving marital bliss on the man alone; he keeps reminding women, through examples of the Prophet's wives (May Allah send abundant blessings and peace upon them), of how they should also behave, in order to maintain peace and happiness within the home.

In this translation, my approach remained semantic, in the sense that I have tried to convey the meanings of the original Arabic text, as best as I could, without compromising the readability and coherence required for an English text. Since this is essentially a book of *seerah*,[1] as it is about the life of the Prophet (ﷺ) with a focus on its domestic aspect, there are numerous hadiths quoted.

I pray to Allah to help us learn from the best mentor of all, the Prophet (ﷺ), and improve ourselves as Muslims. May this book help to return to our families and societies the love, congeniality, and good

---

[1] *seerah*: biography (in this case, of the Prophet)

manners that Allah has created us with, and that Islam nurtures within us.

Finally, I would like to say that this translation is a humble effort on my part, and whatever I have done well is by the grace of Allah. May Allah accept the efforts of all those who contributed to the production of this book, and all praises are for Allah Alone, the Lord of all Worlds.

Najwa Jaffer

Sharjah, United Arab Emirates

In the Name of Allah,
the All Compassionate and All Merciful

Preface

All praises are for Allah alone, the Lord of all worlds. May blessings and peace be upon the most honourable Prophet and Messenger, Muhammad ibn 'Abdullah, who was always truthful and trustworthy. Allah praises His beloved Messenger (*Ṣalla Allâhu 'Alayhi wa Sallam* — Blessings and Peace be upon him) in the following way:

﴿وَمَآ أَرْسَلْنَٰكَ إِلَّا رَحْمَةً لِّلْعَٰلَمِينَ ﴿١٠٧﴾﴾ [الأنبياء: ١٠٧]

﴿And We have not sent you, [O Muhammad], except as a mercy to the worlds.﴾ *(Qur'an 21: 107)*[2]

I ask my Lord to support all of us in doing acts of goodness, abstaining from those that are evil, and nurturing love for the poor in our hearts.

Dear brothers and sisters, the religion of Islam is the greatest blessing that Allah has bestowed upon us. This is because Islam is the religion of the *fiṭrah*.[3] It is the most comprehensive and complete religion, suitable for all times and places. It is the religion of ease, benevolence, and the highest moral standards.

---

[2] Unless otherwise indicated, all translations of the meanings of Qur'anic verses have been adapted from A. Yusuf Ali, *The Meaning of the Holy Qur'an,* 10th ed. or from Saheeh International, *The Qur'an*, (Abul Qasim Publishing House, 1977)

[3] *fiṭrah*: the natural inclination (of humans) instilled by Allah

As an example of this, the guiding principles for a successful married life, which have been laid down for us by Muhammad (ﷺ) are the most beautiful and time-honoured. They encompass gentleness, compassion, co-operation, and wisdom (especially when shown through instances of his own interaction with his wives). I have tried to condense some of these principles into this small book, which begins with a brief introduction to the Prophet's lineage, family, and marital life, and goes on to relate incidences which occurred during this aspect of his outstanding *Sunnah*.[4] The book also contains a short discussion on the issue of polygamy, and disproves common criticisms raised against the Prophet's spotless character due to this aspect of his domestic life. It concludes with a table containing information about his marriages, and a family tree (depicting three generations of the Prophet's offspring).

Surely, writing about such a great personality as the Prophet's, and lifting the screen off the details about his married life, is something that cannot be done thoroughly in just a few volumes or lectures. Hence, it will have to suffice to capture only the essence of this subject within the scope of this book, and leave the rest to be understood by the prudence of the readers.

Today we live in a world, the strangeness of which has exceeded beyond words; tension and anxiety have become rampant within societies, and corruption prevails. It is to our detriment that in today's world, most people are ignorant of the life that was led by our Prophet (ﷺ), and the reason for this is that we have strayed far away from the light and guidance of the Book of Allah and the Sunnah of Muhammad ibn 'Abdullah (blessings and peace be upon him). As a result, small-minded people cross their limits and speak such things

---

[4] *Sunnah*: the practice and collected sayings of Prophet Muhammad (ﷺ) that together with the Qur'an forms the basis of Islamic law

about him as do not suit his dignity. In such sorry circumstances, we bring forth a fragrant bouquet in the form of this book, *The Prophet Muhammad (ﷺ): the best of all husbands,* which will help us to lift the cloak draped around his amazing domestic life, in order to see the compassion, gentleness and justice exhibited in his interactions with his wives. And believe me, if we were aware of these jewels of wisdom, and practised them in our daily lives, so many of our problems would decrease, our homes would be filled with peace, and we would be able to bring forth a generation that would return to the *Ummah*[5] its glorious past. So come along then, into the shady canopy of the Prophet's pure and simple household. Maybe our Lord will bless us with a glimpse of it, allowing us to drink from the hands of His beloved Muhammad (ﷺ) and unite us with him and his wives in the highest garden of Paradise — *Al-Firdaus.* O Allah! Accept this effort as one done purely and sincerely for Your Pleasure. Place it in my balance of good deeds on the day I am laid in my grave. O Allah, Glorified are You above all that is unworthy of You. All praises are for Allah. I bear witness that there is no deity worthy of worship other than Allah, I seek His forgiveness and turn towards Him in repentance.

---

[5] *Ummah*: community or nation: *usu.* used to refer to the entire global community of Muslims

PART ONE

The Prophet's Lineage and His Family

This section consists of two chapters:

Chapter One: The Prophet's lineage

Chapter Two: The Prophet's birth

CHAPTER ONE
The Prophet's lineage

His name was Muhammad, son of 'Abdullah, son of 'Abdul-Muṭṭalib (whose name was Shaybah), son of Hâshim (whose name was 'Amru), son of 'Abd Munâf (whose name was Mugheerah), son of Quṣay (whose name was Zayd), son of Kilâb, son of Murrah, son of Ka'b, son of Lu'ay, son of Ghâlib, son of Fahr (who was given the title 'Al-Quraysh' and their tribe was also named after him). He was the son of Mâlik, son of An-Nud (whose name was Qays), son of Kanânah, son of Khuzaymah, son of Mudrakah (whose name was 'Âmir), son of Ilyâs, son of Mudson of Nizâr, son of Ma'ad, son of 'Adnân.[1]

The Prophet's clan was known as the Hâshimiyah clan, named after his grandfather Hâshim ibn 'Abd Munâf.

Hâshim was the one who took over the responsibility of providing water and money for the pilgrims' food[2] from the sons of 'Abd Munâf, when they made peace with the sons of 'Abd ad-Dâr and divided responsibilities amongst themselves. Hâshim was a very influential and honourable leader. He was the first to feed the pilgrims of Makkah with *thareed.*[3] His name was 'Amru and he was known as Hâshim, because of the bread he would serve. The word

---

[1] Ibn Hisham, 1/1, 2

[2] An amount of money would be kept aside to provide food for the pilgrims who did not have food and/or could not afford it. (Translator)

[3] *thareed*: a dish made from pieces of flat bread soaked in a meat stew

hâshim was derived from *hashm*, which means to break into small pieces, and it refers to his breaking the bread into small pieces (to prepare the meal). He was also the first to establish the two journeys of Quraysh, one in the winter and one in the summer.

'Abdul-Muṭṭalib was the son of 'Abd Munâf (who was an honoured and widely acclaimed leader of his tribe. The Quraysh tribe had given him the title of 'The One who Overflows' due to his generous nature. He was the one to whom the responsibility of providing food and drink to the pilgrims was given after his brother Hâshim passed away.

CHAPTER TWO
The Prophet's birth

The most beloved of the messengers was born in the valley of Banu Hâshim in Makkah, on the morning of Monday, 9th Rabee' al-Awwal in the Islamic calendar. It was the first year after the incident of the elephant, and forty years after the demise of King Chosroes I. This Islamic calendar date coincides with the 20th or 22nd of April, 571 CE according to the great scholar Muhammad Sulaymân al-Mansoor al-Farwee, and the astronomer Maḥmood Pâsha.[1]

Ibn Sa'ad narrates that the mother of Allah's Messenger (ﷺ) said: When I gave birth to him, a light went forth from my womb, which lit up the palaces of Syria. Aḥmad also narrates something similar to this, from Al-'Arbâḍ ibn Sâriyah.[2]

As soon as she gave birth to him, she sent word to his grandfather 'Abdul-Muṭṭalib, giving him the good news of the birth of his grandson. He happily rushed to fetch him and took him inside the Ka'bah, where he prayed to Allah and thanked Him. He named the child Muhammad — which was then an uncommon name amongst the Arabs — and circumcised him on the seventh day, as was customary amongst the Arabs in those days.[3]

---

[1] Al Khuḍree's lectures on the history of Islamic nations 1/62, *'Rahmatul lil alameen'* 1/38-39. Their conflict about the correct date in April stems from their conflict in calibrating the Gregorian calendar.

[2] Ibn Sa'ad 1/63

[3] Ibn Hisham 1/59-60, and Al-Khuḍree's lectures on the history of Islamic=

The first woman who nursed him — after his own mother — was Thuwaybah, the bondswoman of Abu Lahab. She was still nursing her son Masrooḥ and before the Prophet (ﷺ), she had nursed Ḥamzah ibn 'Abdul-Muṭṭalib. Also, after having nursed the Prophet (ﷺ), she nursed Abu Salamah ibn 'Abdul Asad al-Makhzoomee.[4]

It was customary amongst the Arabs of those days to send their children to be nursed by the Bedouin women, away from the ills of the urban cities. This was meant to strengthen their minds and bodies, and to teach them to be eloquent in speech from the very beginning. Hence, 'Abdul-Muṭṭalib also sought a wet-nurse for the Messenger of Allah (ﷺ), and it was a woman from Banu Sa'd ibn Bakr, called Ḥaleemah bint Dhu'ayb and her husband Al-Ḥârith ibn 'Abdul-'Uzzâ al-Maknee from Abu Kabshah of the same tribe, who took charge of him.

Here, the Prophet's foster siblings through nursing were 'Abdullah ibn al-Ḥârith and his sisters Aneesah bint al-Ḥârith and Hudhâfah or Judhâmah bint al-Ḥârith (who was more commonly known as Shaymâ'). Ḥaleemah had also nursed Abu Sufyân ibn al-Ḥârith ibn 'Abdul-Muṭṭalib who was a cousin of the Prophet (ﷺ).

The Prophet's uncle Ḥamzah ibn 'Abdul Muṭṭalib was also being nursed there in Banu Sa'ad ibn Bakr. One day, while the Prophet (ﷺ) was in Ḥaleemah's charge, the nursing mother of Ḥamzah breast-fed Muhammad, and in this way, Ḥamzah became the Prophet's foster brother through nursing from two sides, one being Thuwaybah and the other, Ḥaleemah as-Sa'diyah.[5]

=nations 1/62. However, it is also said that he (ﷺ) was born circumcised. (See: *Talqeeh Fuhoom Ahl al-Athâr* page 4) Ibn al-Qayyim stated that there was no sound hadith regarding this. See: *Zâd al-Ma'âd*, 1/18

[4] *Mukhtasir Seerat ar-Rasool*, by Shaykh 'Abdullah an-Najdi, p. 13

[5] *Zâd al-Ma'âd*, 1/19

PART TWO

The Prophet (ﷺ) With His Wives

This section consists of eight chapters:

Chapter Three: He was patient with his wives

Chapter Four: He was good-natured with his wives

Chapter Five: He would seek the advice of his wives

Chapter Six: He was just with his wives

Chapter Seven: His feelings regarding his wives

Chapter Eight: He was devoted to his wives

Chapter Nine: He was always eager to guide and to help his wives to improve

Chapter Ten: The incident involving the slander against 'Â'ishah and its effect on him

Allah praises his Prophet (ﷺ) saying:

﴿وَإِنَّكَ لَعَلَىٰ خُلُقٍ عَظِيمٍ ﴿٤﴾﴾ [القلم: ٤]

﴾And you [stand] on an exalted standard of character.﴿ *(Qur'an 68: 4)*

These words of Allah in appreciation of His Messenger are enough of an introduction to the personality of the Prophet (ﷺ) and the height of perfection that his manners had attained.

Regarding the special relationship between a husband and his wife, or a family man and his family, the Prophet (ﷺ) said: «The best of you is he who is best to his family, and I am the best of you to my family.»[1]

This shows that the Prophet's yardstick for measuring a person's good manners was how he behaved in his home. Hence, it is not enough that a person acts like an angel outside the home, if after returning home, he becomes a wolf or a tyrannical monster, so to speak. On the contrary, he who practices kindness and forbearance with his children, and is good to his family is more worthy (in the sight of Allah).

Therefore, in this section, we will *inshâ' Allah*[2] shed some light on how the Prophet (ﷺ) conducted himself with his wives.

---

[1] Ibn Mâjah, hadith no. 2008, ruled as a sound hadith by Albâni, in *at-Targheeb wa at-Tarheeb*, (3/72)

[2] *inshâ' Allah:* God willing

CHAPTER THREE
He was patient with his wives

Allah, the Glorified and Exalted has described His beloved Messenger with the words:

﴿لَقَدْ جَآءَكُمْ رَسُولٌ مِّنْ أَنفُسِكُمْ عَزِيزٌ عَلَيْهِ مَا عَنِتُّمْ حَرِيصٌ عَلَيْكُم بِٱلْمُؤْمِنِينَ رَءُوفٌ رَّحِيمٌ ﴿١٢٨﴾﴾ [التوبة: ١٢٨]

﴿Now has come unto you a Messenger from amongst yourselves: it grieves him that you should perish; ardently anxious is he over you; to the Believers he is most kind and merciful. But if they turn away, say: Allah is enough for me: there is none worthy of worship other than He; in Him is my trust; He the Lord of the Throne [of Glory] Supreme!﴾ *(Qur'an 9: 128)*

The qualities of mercy, kindness, and leniency in the Prophet's personality are best exhibited in his relationship with his wives and these can be seen in the following examples:

It is narrated by Anas (رضي الله عنه): «Every night, the Prophet's wives used to collect in the house of the wife whose turn it was. Zaynab (رضي الله عنها) entered 'Â'ishah's house and the Prophet (blessings and peace be upon him) extended his hand, so 'Â'ishah (رضي الله عنها) said: She is Zaynab. So the Prophet (ﷺ) closed his fist, and both (wives) began arguing until their voices became very loud. Abu Bakr, who was passing by, heard them and said: I feel like throwing dirt in their mouths. The time for prayer approached, so the Prophet (ﷺ) got up and left without saying anything to her, but Abu Bakr came back and scolded ‘Â’ishah (may Allah be pleased with her).»[1]

The Prophet’s patience and kindness can be seen in the way he treated his wives here. Even though they were arguing with each other in front of him, he did not rebuke them. An-Nawawi says regarding this:

> ‘I feel like throwing dirt in their mouths’ is an exaggerated expression to scold them and make them stop arguing. Abu Bakr (ﷺ) should be recognized for having the compassion and desire to make peace between the two women, and the hadith[2] shows even more merit on the Prophet’s part for trying to make peace between the wives (by refraining from saying anything).[3]

According to a hadith narrated by ‘Urwah, « ‘Â’ishah (ﷺ) said: The wives of Allah’s Messenger were in two groups. One group consisted of ‘Â’ishah, Ḥafṣah, Ṣafiyah and Sawdah, whilst the other group consisted of Umm Salamah and the rest of the wives. The Muslims knew that the Prophet (ﷺ) loved ‘Â’ishah, so if anyone wanted to give a gift to him, he would delay it until the Prophet (ﷺ) was in ‘Â’ishah’s home, and then he would send his gift to the Prophet (ﷺ) there. The group of Umm Salamah discussed this issue with each other and decided to send Umm Salamah to the Prophet (ﷺ), requesting him to ask the people to send their gifts to him in whichever wife’s house he was. Umm Salamah spoke to him about it, but he did not reply to her. When the wives in her group asked Umm Salamah about it, she said: He did not say anything to me. They told her to try again, so she spoke to him again when he came to her house on her day, but he still did not reply to her. When they asked her, she

---

[1] Muslim, hadith no. 1462

[2] hadith (*ḥadeeth*): a saying or action of Prophet Muhammad (ﷺ) that was remembered and recorded by his Companions and followers

[3] *Sharḥ Muslim* by An-Nawawi, 10/39

told them that he had given no reply. They said to her: Keep asking him till he gives you a reply. Hence, when it was her turn, she talked to him again, and he replied saying: Do not hurt me regarding 'Â'ishah, as the revelation does not come to me on the bed of any other woman other than 'Â'ishah. Upon hearing this, Umm Salamah said: I repent to Allah for hurting you. Then the group of Umm Salamah called Fâṭimah, the Prophet's daughter, and sent her to him, with the message that his wives were requesting him to treat them and the daughter of Abu Bakr on equal terms. Fâṭimah conveyed this message to him. The Prophet (ﷺ) said to Fâṭimah: Don't you love whom I love? She replied in the affirmative, and went back and told the wives about this. They requested her to go back to him again, but she refused. Then they sent Zaynab bint Jaḥsh to him, who went and spoke harshly, saying: Your wives request you to treat them and the daughter of Abu Quhâfah on equal terms. Whilst saying this, she raised her voice and turned to 'Â'ishah, who was sitting there, and insulted her so much that the Prophet (ﷺ) looked at 'Â'ishah to see if she would retort. 'Â'ishah then answered Zaynab back until she had silenced her. The Prophet looked at 'Â'ishah and said: She is truly Abu Bakr's daughter!»[4]

In this hadith, the Prophet (ﷺ) was not being unjust to his other wives on behalf of 'Â'ishah (رضي الله عنها). What his Companions did, they did because they honoured 'Â'ishah (رضي الله عنها) due to the Prophet's love for her. As for the Prophet's attitude towards his wives, it was based on patience and kindness, without being harsh with them, or scolding them for daring to bring this up with him.[5]

Ibn 'Abbâs (رضي الله عنه) narrated: «I spent an entire year, hesitating to ask 'Umar (رضي الله عنه) about the two women who had assisted each other against the Prophet (ﷺ), because I was afraid of him. One day he

---

[4] A sound hadith related by Bukhari

[5] *Al-Ḥayât az-Zawjiyyah min Mindhâr ash-Shar'iyyah*, p. 91

dismounted his riding animal and went among the trees of Arâk to answer the call of nature. When he returned, I asked him about it, and he replied: 'Â'ishah and Ḥafṣah.

'Umar (ﷺ) added: We never gave any importance to women in the days of ignorance,[6] but after the advent of Islam, and upon seeing that Allah Himself mentioned them, we realized that they also have rights upon us. However, we still did not allow them to interfere in our affairs. Once there was a dispute between me and my wife, and she answered back to me in a loud voice. I said to her: Strange! You have come this extent?! She said: You are saying this to me, whilst your own daughter replies to Allah's Messenger (ﷺ) in the same way.

Therefore, I went to Ḥafṣah (ﷺ) and said to her: I warn you not to disobey Allah and His Messenger. Then I went to Umm Salamah (ﷺ) and told her the same. She, however, replied to me, saying: O 'Umar! It surprises me to see that you keep interfering in our affairs so much so that you are now meddling into the personal affairs of the Prophet and his wives. Hence, she rejected my advice.

There was a man amongst the Helpers,[7] with whom I had an arrangement, that whenever he was absent and I was with the Prophet (ﷺ), I would tell him about what had happened that day, and when I was absent and he was present, he would tell me about what had happened. At that time, all the rulers of the nearby lands had surrendered to the Prophet (ﷺ) except the Syrian King of Ghassân, from whom we feared an impending attack. All of a sudden, that man from the Helpers came and said: A catastrophe has occurred! I asked him: What is it? Has the Ghasâni (King) come? He said: Worse than

---

[6] The period before the advent of Islam is often referred to as 'the days of ignorance'. (Editor)

[7] Helpers: (in Arabic, *Anṣâr*) the Muslim citizens of Madinah who gave refuge to the Prophet (ﷺ) and the other Muslim emigrants from Makkah

that! Allah's Messenger has divorced his wives! I went to see and heard the sound of crying coming from the houses of all of the wives. I was told that the Prophet had ascended to an upper room of his. At the door of that room, there was a slave to whom I went and said: Seek the Prophet's permission to allow me to enter. He allowed me in, and I went in to see that the Prophet was lying on a mat. The mat had left an imprint on his side. Under his head was a leather pillow stuffed with palm fibres. There were some hides hanging there and some grasses used for tanning. I mentioned to him what I had said to Ḥafṣah and Umm Salamah, and the reply that Umm Salamah had given to me. Upon hearing it, Allah's Messenger laughed. He (ﷺ) stayed there for twenty-nine days and then came down.»[8]

Notice the magnificent patience that the Prophet (ﷺ) displayed in this issue. When 'Umar's wife retorted to her husband over some issues, 'Umar took it as a great offence; yet the Prophet's wives were used to answering him back, arguing with him and having discussions with him, and he would calmly listen to them without denying them this indulgence. This shows the humility, mercy, and kindness with which he dealt with his wives. In fact, he was so kind and patient with his wives that they would talk back to him and abandon him until night came, but he would remain patient and forgiving with them.

It is narrated by Nu'mân ibn Basheer (رضي الله عنه):

«Abu Bakr (رضي الله عنه) came and sought permission to enter the Prophet's house. He heard 'Â'ishah (رضي الله عنها) raising her voice over that of the Prophet's. After being permitted, he entered, got hold of her, and said: O daughter of Umm Roomân, why are you raising your voice over that of the Messenger of Allah? The Prophet (ﷺ) intervened and prevented him from hitting his daughter. When Abu Bakr (رضي الله عنه) left, the Prophet (ﷺ) consoled her and said: Did you see how I saved you

---

[8] Related by Bukhari: a sound hadith

from him? After a while, Abu Bakr (رضي الله عنه) returned, sought permission to enter, and this time he saw the Prophet (ﷺ) joking and laughing with 'Â'ishah (رضي الله عنها). Abu Bakr (رضي الله عنه) said: O Messenger of Allah, allow me to be part of your peace, just as you have allowed me to be part of your conflict.»[9]

This is where many people mistakenly think that life after marriage is like a little heaven for the two spouses, where not even a shadow of problems and conflicts could appear. In reality, the opposite is true, and Allah's way is to test humankind through many different kinds of trials:

﴿ٱلَّذِى خَلَقَ ٱلْمَوْتَ وَٱلْحَيَوٰةَ لِيَبْلُوَكُمْ أَيُّكُمْ أَحْسَنُ عَمَلًا ۚ وَهُوَ ٱلْعَزِيزُ ٱلْغَفُورُ ﴿٢﴾﴾

[المُلك: ٢]

﴾He Who created Death and Life, that He may try which of you is best in deed; and He is the Exalted in Might, Oft-Forgiving.﴿

(Qur'an 67: 2)

Furthermore, the patience of the Messenger of Allah can also be seen through this hadith.

«The Prophet was sent some food (by one of his other wives, whilst he was in 'Â'ishah's house). 'Â'ishah came and struck the hand of the servant, which caused the dish to fall and break, (spilling the food on the floor). The Prophet (ﷺ) gathered the broken pieces of the dish, collected in them the remnants of the spilt food, and said to those present: Eat, your mother became jealous, your mother became jealous.»

This hadith serves as a good reminder for us all, teaching us how the Prophet (ﷺ) used to interact with his wives. May Allah send blessings and peace upon our Prophet Muhammad (ﷺ), and upon all of his family and Companions.

---

[9] Related by Ahmed, graded as *ḥasan* (good)

CHAPTER FOUR
He was good-natured with his wives

Unlike many husbands, our Prophet (ﷺ) was not a man who was dominating and selfish at home, aggressively forcing his opinions on others, with an incessant frown on his face all the while. Instead, he set an example by being extremely good-natured and friendly with his family.

His cheerful nature is also shown from the Hadith in which he gives Â'ishah a nickname — 'Ayesh: «'Â'ishah (رضي الله عنها) narrated that the Prophet (ﷺ) said to her: O 'Âyesh! This is Gabriel here, conveying his greetings of peace to you. She replied: May the peace and mercy of Allah be upon him too.»[1]

Â'ishah (رضي الله عنها) narrated another hadith: «I went with the Prophet (ﷺ) on one of his journeys, whilst I was still a slim and slender young girl. He instructed the others to go on without us, and they went on ahead. Then, he said to me: Come, let's race. I raced with him and won the race. Then he never mentioned it again, and I had even forgotten about it, until one day I was accompanying him on another one of his journeys. By now, I was older and had become heavier. As before, he instructed his Companions to go ahead without us, and they went on ahead. Then he said to me: Come, let's race. And this time he won the race. He laughed and said: This is to make

[1] Muslim, hadith no. 2447

up (for my last defeat).»[2]

Qaḍi 'Iyâḍ, may Allah have mercy upon him, said:

> This hadith demonstrates that certain forms of entertainment are permissible, and it also shows how courteous and big-hearted he was in his domestic life.[3]

According to an authentic narration:

«It is narrated by 'Â'ishah (ﷺ) that Abu Bakr (ﷺ) entered upon her whilst she was with two of her friends on the day of Mina. They were playing the tambourine and singing songs, whilst the Prophet (ﷺ) was lying down with his face covered with his cloth. Abu Bakr rebuked them, so the Prophet (ﷺ) uncovered his face and said: Let her be, O Abu Bakr, it's Eid. ('Â'ishah added:) I have seen the Prophet (ﷺ) screen me with his cloth, allowing me to see the Abyssinians play, and I was a young girl; so treat the young girl according to her age, as she is playful, spirited and youthful.»[4]

Her words, 'so treat the young girl according to her age' mean that young girls like to look at and enjoy activities of leisure and entertainment, and hence, their husbands (or fathers) should take care of this desire of theirs and allow them to enjoy it until they are satisfied.[5]

This hadith shows how kind, merciful, and indulgent the Prophet (ﷺ) was with his wives and in his social interactions with them.

This marvellous religion of Islam is characterized by its ease and leniency, as it caters to the needs of a human being, whatever his

---

[2] Ibn Mâjah, hadith no. 2010, ruled as a sound hadith by Albâni, in *Al-'Irwâ'*

[3] *Al-Fatḥ al-Bâri*, 1/549

[4] Muslim, hadith no. 892

[5] *Sharḥ Muslim* by An-Nawawi (6/490)

or her circumstances or situation. Despite the fact that the reason for our existence on this planet is to worship Allah, there is nothing wrong with having fun and being merry, as long as it does not go against the limits set by Islam.[6]

The following hadith shows us how the Prophet (ﷺ) would teach and encourage his wives to revitalize their marriage, and not let it become dull, monotonous, or lacking in novelty. Therefore, marital life should not only be about eating, drinking and doing the washing. It is the husband's duty to play with his wife and joke with her, because having fun together cements the marital relationship as nothing else does.

«'Â'ishah (رضي الله عنها) narrated: Sawdah visited us one day, and sat with one leg in my room and the other in her own. I prepared a meal called *khazeerah*[7] and said to her: Eat. She refused, so I took some of the food and smeared it on her face. The Prophet (ﷺ) laughed and raised his leg, which was in her part of the house, in order to help her get back at me. He said to her: You smear her face (now). So she took some of the food from the plate and smeared my face with it, and the Prophet (ﷺ) laughed.»[8]

---

[6] *At-Tarweeḥ at-Tarbawee Ru'yah Islâmiyah*, p. 27

[7] *khazeerah:* a dish prepared by cutting meat into small pieces and covering it with water. When the meat is almost done, some flour is sprinkled on to it (and cooked for a while).

[8] An-Nasâ'ee, hadith no. 8917. It was collected by Abu Ya'lâ, with a good narration (4496). According to its researcher Husayn Muslim, the narration is *ḥasan*, and something similar is recorded in *Majma'a az-Zâyid* by Al-Haythamee (4/316). He said: It was narrated by Abu Ya'lâ, whose narrators were sound, except Muhammad ibn 'Umar, whose hadith is *ḥasan*.

CHAPTER FIVE
He would seek the advice of his wives

Some husbands look down upon their wives, considering them inferior in intellect and understanding. They never seek their wife's advice on any important issue of their life because they do not think she is worthy of giving any intelligent advice. However, the Prophet (ﷺ), being a model for all Muslims, found nothing wrong in seeking the advice of his wife Umm Salamah (رضي الله عنها) regarding an extremely sensitive and important political issue.

«(At Ḥudaybiyah) the Prophet (ﷺ) said to his Companions: Get up, take off your *iḥrâm*[1] and shave (your heads). (The narrator says:) By Allah! Not a single man got up, even after the Prophet (ﷺ) had repeated himself thrice. Thereafter, he went to his wife Umm Salamah and related to her how the people were acting. She said to him: Do you really want this? (If yes,) then go out, and without saying a word to any of them, take off your own *iḥrâm*, and ask your barber to shave your head. Therefore, he went out, and without saying a word to any of them, took off his pilgrim's garb, and got his head shaved. When the people saw this, they got up, took off their pilgrim's garb, and began shaving each other's heads with such vigour that it seemed they would almost kill each other whilst doing it.»[2]

---

[1] *iḥrâm*: the special clothing worn by the pilgrim on the Hajj or 'umrah, signifying the state of consecration

[2] Bukhari, hadith no. 2731

Ibn Hajr explained this hadith, saying, "It shows that it is good to seek advice and that it is allowed to seek the advice of a capable woman." The Imam of the Two Sacred Mosques said: "We do not know of any other woman other than Umm Salamah, who gave advice and it was acted upon."[3]

It is also worth mentioning here that there are some fabricated hadiths, which demean the status of women and their opinions. Scholars have warned people to be wary of these fabricated hadiths. Some of them are, 'Obeying the wife (leads to) regret,' and 'Seek their advice, then do the opposite of what they say.' Also, 'There are three whom if you obey them, you will be disgraced: the slave, the wife and the farmer.'[4] Such inauthentic hadiths obviously go against the Qur'an and the Sunnah.

---

[3] *Fatḥ al-Bâri,* 5/347

[4] *Kashf al-khafâ wa muzeel ul-ilbâs 'alâ al-aḥâdeeth al-mushtahirah 'alâ alsinat an-nâs,* 2/14

CHAPTER SIX

He was just with his wives

The justice and equality displayed in the Prophet's relationship with all his wives (may Allah be pleased with them) was exemplary, even though Allah had revealed this verse to him:

﴿تُرْجِي مَن تَشَآءُ مِنْهُنَّ وَتُـْٔوِىٓ إِلَيْكَ مَن تَشَآءُ ۖ وَمَنِ ٱبْتَغَيْتَ مِمَّنْ عَزَلْتَ فَلَا
جُنَاحَ عَلَيْكَ ۚ ذَٰلِكَ أَدْنَىٰٓ أَن تَقَرَّ أَعْيُنُهُنَّ وَلَا يَحْزَنَّ وَيَرْضَيْنَ بِمَآ ءَاتَيْتَهُنَّ
كُلُّهُنَّ ۚ وَٱللَّهُ يَعْلَمُ مَا فِى قُلُوبِكُمْ ۚ وَكَانَ ٱللَّهُ عَلِيمًا حَلِيمًا ﴿٥١﴾﴾

[الأحزاب: ٥١]

﴿You may defer [the turn of] any of them that you wish, and you may receive any that you wish, and there is no blame on you if you invite one whose [turn] you had set aside. This is better, that they may be comforted and not grieve, and may be satisfied — all of them — with what you give them: and Allah knows [all] that is in your hearts: and Allah is All-Knowing, Most Forbearing.﴾ *(Qur'an 33: 51)*

Muhammad Rasheed Râza explained this Qur'anic verse saying:

> Through this verse, Allah removed from His Prophet (ﷺ) the restrictions that He had placed upon the rest of the Ummah, in terms of the strict observance of fairness and equality with one's wives. Allah permitted him (ﷺ) to keep in waiting, which ever of his wives he wished to delay, to stay with

whichever of them he wished, and to stay away from any of them if he wanted to. In spite of this, the Prophet (ﷺ) continued to treat them with equality and justice, as he was used to doing.[1]

«Even during his final illness, when it became difficult for him to move each day from one wife's house to the others, as he would during his health, he would ask: Where will I be tomorrow? Where will I be tomorrow? (seeking 'Â'ishah's turn).»[2]

It is true that the Prophet (ﷺ) loved 'Â'ishah (رضي الله عنها) the most, due to her beauty, intelligence, youth, and the fact that she was Abu Bakr's daughter. It should be clear that he did not love her more because he considered the other wives to be of low intellect or lineage, and nor did he ever differentiate between them with regards to how much he spent on them, how many nights he slept with them, or how he behaved with them.

Furthermore, in spite of how much he loved 'Â'ishah (رضي الله عنها), the Prophet (ﷺ) never refrained from correcting her when she misbehaved with any of the other wives, as we can see from the hadith in which Umm Salamah (رضي الله عنها) sent a meal she had prepared, and when 'Â'ishah (رضي الله عنها) came and (in her anger and jealousy) flipped over the dish containing the food, the Prophet (ﷺ) made her give one of her own dishes in compensation for Umm Salamah's dish, which she had broken.[3]

The great stance of justice and equality that the Prophet (ﷺ) took here is worth contemplating.

---

[1] *Ḥuqooq an-Nisâ' fil-Islâm*

[2] Bukhari, Book of the Battles, 8/144

[3] Bukhari, hadith no. 5252

«Once, out of jealousy, 'Â'ishah (رضي الله عنها) criticized Ṣafiyah (رضي الله عنها), saying: O Messenger of Allah, have you noticed how short Ṣafiyah is? He replied: Indeed you have said something (so bad) that if it were mixed into the sea, it would pollute the entire sea.»[4]

The two hadiths above illustrate the beautiful manners of the Prophet (ﷺ), especially regarding how fair he was to each of his wives, and this serves as an example for all husbands, teaching them how to be just and fair in their dealings with their wives.

---

[4] At-Tirmidhi, hadith no. 2502: a *ḥasan ṣaḥeeḥ* (i.e., a grade between good and sound) narration

CHAPTER SEVEN
His feelings regarding his wives

Indeed our Prophet Muhammad (ﷺ) possessed beautiful qualities like that of mercy, kindness, and consideration for others' feelings, which were all evident in his interaction with his wives. While reading the hadiths about his domestic life, you will see him being indulgent with one wife due to her young age, being sensitive to the feelings of another, or affectionately paying attention to another's words until she finished speaking, and so on and so forth. These high standards of moral conduct exemplified in his personality prove to us with great clarity the difference between our own marital interactions and those of our Prophet (ﷺ).

At-Tirmidhi related a hadith of Anas ibn Mâlik (رضي الله عنه): «Ṣafiyah narrated that Ḥafṣah once said to her: You Jew! This made Ṣafiyah cry, and while she was crying, the Prophet (ﷺ) came in. He asked her what the matter was. She told him: Ḥafṣah called me a Jew. The Prophet (ﷺ) said to her: You are the daughter of a prophet (Aaron), your uncle (Moses) was a prophet, and now you are the wife of a prophet. You have much to be proud of. Then he said (to Ḥafṣah): Fear Allah, O Ḥafṣah.»[1]

«It is narrated from 'Â'ishah (رضي الله عنها) that (while they were on a journey) Ṣafiyah's camel collapsed, and Zaynab (رضي الله عنها) had many camels, so the Prophet (ﷺ) said to her: Ṣafiyah's camel has

---

[1] At-Tirmidhi, hadith no. 3894; authenticated by Al-Albâni in *Mishkât al-Maṣâbeeḥ*, 2/358

collapsed, so could you give her one of your camels? She said: (You expect) me to give (a camel) to that Jewish woman? The Prophet (ﷺ) left Zaynab and showed his displeasure with her by staying away from her for two or three months, until she folded up her bed, and began thinking that he would never forgive her. 'Â'ishah (رضي الله عنها) says: I was with him one day, when at midday, he entered (her apartment), and she put her bedding back in its place.»[2]

According to a hadith narrated by 'Â'ishah (رضي الله عنها), when the Prophet (ﷺ) married her she was a girl of six, and when he consummated the marriage, she was nine years old. She was used to playing with her friends with dolls made of cotton, as is the norm with girls of that age. When the Prophet (ﷺ) used to enter, her friends would hide, but the Prophet (ﷺ) would tell 'Â'ishah (رضي الله عنها) to go to them and continue their play.[3]

Can there be a greater show of consideration for the feelings of a wife, her age, and her vulnerabilities than this? Furthermore, once the Prophet (ﷺ) delayed an entire army, in order to look for a bracelet of Asmâ's which had been lost by 'Â'ishah (رضي الله عنها).[4]

Such qualities lead to marital bliss within the Muslim household. The key to establishing a good marital relationship and keeping a marriage within safe waters is to know each other's nature and to have consideration for each other's feelings.

The following hadith narrated by Asmâ' bint Abu Bakr (رضي الله عنه) shows us that it is equally important for the wife to show consideration for her husband's feelings:

---

[2] Ahmad, hadith no. 1699, 25718. Al-Albâni grades it as a *ḥasan* narration in his book *At-Targheeb wat-Tarheeb.*

[3] Muslim, hadith no. 81 & 4939

[4] Muslim, hadith no. 367

«When I got married to Az-Zubayr (رضي الله عنه), he owned nothing but a camel which drew water from a well and a horse. I used to feed the horse its fodder and drew water from the well. I sewed the bucket which was used to draw out the water. I also kneaded the dough, but since I did not know how to bake the bread, my *Anṣâri*[5] neighbours would bake it for me. They were honourable women. I also used to carry the date-stones on my head, all the way from Az-Zubayr's land, which was given to him by the Prophet (ﷺ), to our home, which was about two miles away. One day, while I was walking home with the date-stones on my head, I met the Messenger of Allah who was accompanied with some men from amongst the Helpers. He called out to me and made his camel kneel down, saying: Ikh! Ikh! and beckoning me to ride behind him on his camel. I felt shy of going with the men, and I also remembered Az-Zubayr's sense of jealousy and possessiveness. He was an extremely jealous and possessive man. Allah's Messenger (ﷺ) noticed my hesitation and moved on. Later, when I met Az-Zubayr, I told him: I met Allah's Messenger when I was on my way back, carrying a load of date-stones on my head. He (ﷺ) was accompanied by some of his Companions, and he made his camel kneel down, so as to help me climb up behind him, but I felt shy in his presence, and also remembered your sense of jealousy.

Upon hearing this, Az-Zubayr said: By Allah! Your carrying the date-stones [and then being seen by the Prophet (ﷺ) in such a state] is more shameful to me than your riding on his camel. (Asmâ' added:) I kept doing the same work until Abu Bakr finally sent me a servant, who then looked after the horse, after which I felt as if I had been set free (manumitted).»[6]

---

[5] *Anṣâri*: the adjectival form of *Anṣâr*: 'helpers': the Muslim citizens of Madinah who gave refuge to the Prophet (ﷺ) and the other Muslim emigrants from Makkah

[6] Muslim, hadith no. 2182

In this hadith, we can see how this pious woman who knew her husband's jealous nature, showed such immense consideration for his feelings, that she refused the offer for a ride by the Prophet (ﷺ) himself, out of fear of displeasing her husband. This alone holds great lessons for every Muslim woman who desires to please Allah and succeed in the hereafter. It teaches us that if a woman knows that her husband dislikes something, or gets offended by something, then it is not permissible for her to go against his wishes and do anything that would displease him and make him upset. It would be wrong of her to do so, because it may be that her husband is her only key to entering Paradise, or at least one of the keys, as is mentioned in this hadith: «Look at where you stand, by the way your husband feels about you, for indeed he is your Heaven and he is your Hell.»[7]

The husband's place is very high in Islam, and taking his likes and dislikes seriously is something that comes naturally to the believing woman whose eyes are fixed on her prize, that is to say, Paradise. In the same way, it is also obligatory for the husband to be considerate of his wife's feelings, especially when she is pregnant, after giving birth, and during her menstrual cycles, because taking care of her in such times would show how much he cares for her and his family.

Similarly, it is also necessary for the husband to listen to his wife attentively, because being able to listen to one another with attention is actually the highest example of showing consideration and respect for each other. Such good listening skills were also a characteristic of our Prophet Muhammad (ﷺ), who listened to 'Â'ishah (رضي الله عنها) tell the tale of the eleven women with so much attention, that at the end of it, he was able to say something to her, which won her heart and filled her with peace and happiness. All

[7] Ibn Abee Shaibah, Hadith No.1, 47/170; authenticated by Al-Albani

this shows how beautifully he interacted with his wives, showing sensitivity to the other person's feelings and thoughts. 'Â'ishah (may Allah be pleased with her) narrated this authentic hadith as follows:

«[I told the Messenger of Allah (ﷺ) this parable:] Eleven women sat together and promised each other that they would not conceal from each other anything about their husbands. The first one said: My husband is like the meat of a lean camel which is kept on the top of a rocky mountain. This mountain is not easy to climb, nor is the meat (that you get from it) fleshy, so that one might put up with the trouble of fetching it.[8] The second one said: I shall not relate my husband's qualities, for I fear that I may not be able to finish his story, for if I try to think of him, all that comes to mind is his facial and abdominal veins. The third one said: My husband is a tall man;[9] if I describe him (and he hears of that) he will divorce me, and if I keep quiet, he will neither divorce me nor treat me as a wife. The fourth one said: My husband is a moderate person like the sort of night which is neither hot nor cold. I am neither afraid of him, nor am I discontented (or bored) with him.[10] The fifth one said: My husband, when entering (the house) is a leopard, and when going out, is a lion.

[8] She is criticizing her husband, by saying that his flesh is like the flesh of a weak and puny camel. It implies that she does not enjoy her relationship with her husband. He is a weak man, without much flesh, and her conjugal relationship with her husband is being referred to here. She does not enjoy him physically, and to make matters worse, his personality is defective. He is hard to talk to, and after all her sufferings, when she does get to him, the wife wonders what she gains in this relationship.

[9] i.e. he is tall or maybe the list of his bad qualities is long. It is said: this refers to an ill-mannered man.

[10] This wife describes her marital life as one of peace and happiness. She does not feel any fear or boredom in her life with him, and she compares herself to the people who enjoy the coolness, ease, and pleasantness of the evening.=

He does not ask about what is in the house.[11] The sixth one said: When my husband eats, he eats too much, and when he drinks, he leaves nothing, and if he sleeps, he sleeps curled up and does not stretch his hands here and there so as to know how I fare.[12] The seventh one said: My husband is a fool[13] or a eunuch,[14] and at the height of idiocy.[15] All the defects are present in him. If you talk to him, you may end up injuring your head, your body, or both.[16] The eighth one said: My husband is as soft to touch as a rabbit and smells

---

=Thus, she enjoys her life with him, because of his excellent companionship and the moderation in his personality, and Allah knows best.

[11] He does not ask about what he sees in the house. The way this woman has described her husband, could have two possible interpretations; the first is that she is praising her husband, saying that when he enters the home, he approaches her (eagerly) like a leopard. He is very attracted to her and cannot resist his urge, as soon as he sets eyes upon her. In addition, when he goes out in public, he is as brave as a lion. He generously provides her with food, drink, and clothes, without asking her about where and how she spent them. The alternative meaning could be that she is criticizing her husband, by saying that when he enters the home, he is like a leopard: he does not exchange any pleasantries with her before making love to her. Furthermore, he is ill mannered and abuses her physically and verbally. He does not ask her how she is; she may be sick, but he will not care about and ask her about how she is feeling or how her children are doing.

[12] She describes her husband, saying that he is gluttonous and thinks so much of food and drink, that it is never enough for him. When he sleeps, he wraps himself in his blankets and sleeps away from her, which makes her melancholic and depressed. Furthermore, he does not even reach out to her to find out why she is upset, and this increases her despair. Allah knows best.

[13] i.e. weak and sinful

[14] i.e. unable to have sexual intercourse with women

[15] i.e. he has reached the height of foolishness

[16] This vice of foolishness in him, makes him not just unable to fulfil her needs and desires, but also causes her harm. When she tries to talk to him, he shuts her up, hits her, thus hurting her both physically and emotionally. In this way, he does not leave out a single part of her body (and soul) which he has not harmed, and Allah knows best.

like sweet herbs.[17] The ninth one said: My husband has tall pillars,[18] and has a long sheath (for his sword).[19] His ashes are abundant and his house is open to the people.[20] The tenth one said: My husband is Mâlik, and what is Mâlik? Mâlik is better than that.[21] Most of his camels are kept at home (ready to be slaughtered for the guests) and only a few are taken to the pastures. When the camels hear the sound of the lute (or the tambourine)[22] they realize that they are going to be slaughtered for the guests. The eleventh one said: My husband is Abu Zar' and what is Abu Zar' (that is to say, what should I say about him?). My ears jingled with earrings,[23] and my arms grew plump. He honoured me, increasing me in self-confidence, and made me feel proud of myself. He found me with my family who were mere owners of sheep and living in poverty, and brought me to a respected family, who owned horses, camels, cattle and poultry, and threshed and purified grain.[24] Whatever I said, he did not rebuke me.[25] When I

---

[17] She praises her husband for how well he beautifies and perfumes himself for her. Allah knows best.

[18] i.e. his house is tall and spacious, like those of the nobility, honourable people, and to which guests always come.

[19] i.e. he is brave and courageous.

[20] i.e. people go to him with their problems and pleas. She praises her husband for the grandeur of his house, which is like the house of the nobles. He is tall and requires a long sheath, which points towards his bravery and gallantry. He is a generous man, which is why his fire is always burning (making his house always warm and welcoming to people). His house is always open means that he is always available to the people, who can easily approach him with their problems, and Allah knows best.

[21] i.e. he is better than all those who have been mentioned before him.

[22] This musical instrument used to be played in the days of ignorance, in order to welcome and honour guests.

[23] He bought her so many earrings, that her ears were loaded with them, and one could hear them jingle.

[24] i.e. he made her wealthy.

[25] Whatever she might say to him, he did not curse her or scold her. He=

slept, I slept until late in the morning.[26] When I drank, (water or milk), I drank my fill. The mother of Abu Zar' — and what may one say in praise of the mother of Abu Zar'? Her saddlebags[27] were always full of provision and her house was spacious.[28] As for the son of Abu Zar' — what may one say about the son of Abu Zar'? His bed was like the stick drawn out of a mat of dried palm leaves,[29] and his hunger could be satisfied with just the shank of a small female goat.[30] As for the daughter of Abu Zar', she was obedient to both her father and her mother. Her garment was wholesome,[31] and she aroused the jealousy of her neighbours.[32] As for the maidservant of Abu Zar' — what may one say of the maidservant of Abu Zar'? She did not divulge our secrets but kept them to herself. She did not waste our provisions[33] and did not leave the rubbish scattered in our

---

=honoured her, and thereby spoiled her (lovingly).

[26] She did not need to wake up early to begin her chores of the day, and this implies that there were enough servants to carry out the tasks of the household.

[27] A saddlebag implies the place where she stored her possessions.

[28] Her house was extremely spacious, and contained an abundance of furniture, food, and clothes. She owned a lot of wealth and lived a life of great ease and comfort.

[29] She praises Abu Zar''s son, saying that the place he slept in was as small as a single stick taken out of a whole mat made of dried palm leaves, i.e. he did not occupy a large part of the house.

[30] She implies that he was of small build and did not eat a lot. Hence, she says that her husband's son was not a burden upon her.

[31] This phrase implies that she had a good personality and a beautiful body.

[32] Her women neighbours felt jealous of her when they saw her blessings and bounties. Her women neighbours here may be referring to her co-wives or to her actual neighbours, as 'Umar (رضي الله عنه) once said to his daughter Ḥafsah (may Allah be pleased with them both): «Do not be jealous if your neighbour outshines you. [implying 'Â'ishah (رضي الله عنها)].»

[33] Neither did she steal any of their things, nor did she let them spoil or go to waste.

house.[34] The eleventh lady added: One day, it so happened that Abu Zar‘ went out at the time when the animals were being milked,[35] and he saw a woman who had two sons. The two sons were like two leopards playing with the two pomegranates (breasts) above her waist.[36] (On seeing her) he divorced me and married her.[37] Thereafter, I married a noble man who used to ride a fast, tireless horse and keep a spear in his hand.[38] He gave me many things, and also a pair of every kind of livestock and said: Eat (of this), O Umm Zar‘, and also give to your relatives.[39] She added: Yet, all the things which my second husband gave me could not fill the smallest utensil of Abu Zar‘'s. ‘Â'ishah (رضي الله عنها) then said: Allah's Messenger (ﷺ) said to me: I am to you as Abu Zar‘ was to his wife Umm Zar‘.»[40]

The following is one of the most beautiful hadiths that shows us how much the Prophet (ﷺ) cared about the feelings of others:

---

[34] She liked cleanliness and kept their house neat and tidy.

[35] This milk was to be used to make butter and cream.

[36] One day Abu Zar‘ left home early, at the a time when the servants and slaves were busy in their chores. It was the season of mating, during spring time, and this is probably why he saw this woman in this particular state. She had been churning the milk, when she got tired and decided to take some rest, by feeding her two sons from her breasts. This is when Abu Zar‘ saw her, and it seemed to him that her two sons were like two leopards, drinking her milk.

[37] Men in those days used to prefer fertile women, and this is why he desired her when he saw her sons playing with her breasts. Hence, he married her, but she did not stay with him until he had divorced Umm Zar‘.

[38] She married a kind, generous and honourable gentleman, who owned many horses.

[39] This shows how generous and big-hearted he was. However, in spite of this, she says: Even if I collected all the things my second husband gave me, they would be unable to fill even a single utensil of Abu Zar‘'s. This shows that her love for Abu Zar‘ still occupied her heart. (*Sharḥ Muslim* by An-Nawawi, 568).

[40] Muslim, hadith no. 2448

«It is narrated by 'Â'ishah (﵂) that the Prophet (ﷺ) said: I know when you are pleased with me and when you are not. She asked: How do you know that? He replied: When you are pleased with me, you say: No, by the Lord of Muhammad; and when you are not pleased with me, you say: No, by the Lord of Abraham. Thereupon, she said: Yes, but, by Allah, O Messenger of Allah, I did not abandon anything except your name.»

Ibn Ḥajr (may Allah have mercy upon him) said regarding his words, 'I know when you are pleased with me':

> It shows that a man should be able to deduce his wife's emotional state from her words and actions, especially with regards to her pleasure or displeasure with him.

Ibn Ḥajr commented further on this hadith, saying:

> Her words: 'I did not abandon anything except your name,' are immensely sweet, because through these words, she informs her husband that even when she is in a state of anger, in which a person loses control over his or her mind, no change comes to her unwavering love for him.[41]

The biography of our Prophet Muhammad (ﷺ) is worth studying, as it is full of beautiful examples of good conduct and the best of etiquettes. May Allah send blessings and peace upon His Messenger Muhammad, his family and honourable Companions.

Wiping the tears of his wife Ṣafiyah (﵂):

«Ṣafiyah bint Ḥuyay narrated that the Prophet (ﷺ) performed Hajj with his womenfolk. At some points during their journey, a man would descend from his riding animal, and would steer the animals to

[41] *Fatḥ al-Bâri*, 9/345

quicken their pace. Hence, the Prophet (ﷺ) told him to hurry up the 'vessels' (implying the women). As the riding animals of the women started moving faster, the camel of Ṣafiyah bint Ḥuyay knelt down and overthrew her. She was the most sensitive of all of them, and she began to cry. When the Prophet (ﷺ) found out, he came to her and wiped her tears with his own hands, upon which she started to cry even more. The Prophet (ﷺ) told her not to cry but she became even more fitful and began crying inconsolably. So he ordered the people to dismount, even though he had not wanted to dismount, and the caravan dismounted. Ṣafiyah explained: The caravan dismounted whilst it was my turn with the Prophet (ﷺ). As the people dismounted, the Prophet (ﷺ) set up his tent and entered it. I was not sure what this meant,[42] and I feared that he may be a little upset with me, so I went to 'Â'ishah (رضي الله عنها) and said to her: You know very well that I would not trade my turn with the Prophet (ﷺ) for anything whatsoever, but I am giving you my turn, only to gain back his pleasure. 'Â'ishah (رضي الله عنها) replied: Yes. 'Â'ishah (رضي الله عنها) then took a garment of hers, brushed it with saffron, and sprinkled it with water to refresh its fragrance. Then she wore it, and went to the Prophet's tent, and raised the curtain. He said to her: What is it 'Â'ishah? It is not your day. She replied: This is the bounty of Allah; He gives to whom He wills.»[43]

The stance of the beloved Muhammad (ﷺ) was most thoughtful and considerate, as he wiped his wife's tears with his own hands, and ordered the people to stop their journey and dismount, although he himself did not want to get down, but he did so for the sake of his wife. On the other hand, look how concerned the wife was, about having possibly displeased her husband, that she exchanged her turn with 'Â'ishah (رضي الله عنها) in order to win back his pleasure.

---

[42] He went in all of a sudden, without telling anyone.

[43] *Musnad Ahmad*, hadith no. 2/143-144

This small story contains countless lessons and benefits for couples who wish to live a happily married life. Spouses should have this goal in mind (that they will try to do that which pleases their spouse, even if it goes against their own wishes), and should persevere with it as if it is a code for their marital life, in order to fill their lives with peace and happiness.

Wiping the tears of one's wife is taken as the best way to comfort and support a wife, because it shows that the husband is validating her emotions and feelings. This is especially true when, in the husband's view, the wife is crying over something very petty, and to shed tears over a light fall from the camel only shows a very delicate nature. However, the Prophet (ﷺ) did not invalidate Ṣafiyah's feelings or scorn her for crying over something so trivial. Instead, he respected her feelings, consoled her, and made the whole caravan stop and dismount, for her sake alone. Indeed, he knew that tears are tremendously precious and sacred things, especially if their value is understood by both parties.

Imam Bukhari mentions two incidents, both of which took place between the Prophet (ﷺ) and his wife Ṣafiyah bint Ḥuyay, and which further show how cordial and respectful he (ﷺ) was with his wives:

'Ali ibn al-Ḥusayn (رضي الله عنه) narrated this hadith: «The Prophet's wife, Ṣafiyah (رضي الله عنها) told me that once she went to meet the Prophet (ﷺ) in the mosque, whilst he was in *'itikâf* [44] during the last ten days of Ramadan. She talked to him for a while, after which she got up to leave. The Prophet (ﷺ) also got up to walk her home. As they reached the gate of the mosque, opposite Umm Salamah's door, two men from amongst the Helpers passed them by, and the Prophet (ﷺ) greeted them. He said to them: Do not run away! She is (my wife)

---

[44] *itikâf:* seclusion in the mosque solely for the purpose of worship

Ṣafiyah bint Ḥuyay. They both exclaimed: *Subḥân Allâh*![45] (How could we even dare to think any evil?) O Messenger of Allah. And they meant it. The Prophet (ﷺ) said to them: Satan runs through a human's veins like blood. I feared that Satan might whisper an evil thought into your minds.»[46]

Anas ibn Mâlik (رضي الله عنه) narrated the following hadith:

«The Prophet (ﷺ) came to Khaybar and conquered the fortified town after gaining victory in the battle, by breaking down the enemy's defences. There, the beauty of Ṣafiyah bint Ḥuyay (رضي الله عنها) was mentioned to him. Her husband had been killed (in that battle), and she was still a bride. The Prophet (ﷺ) chose her for himself, and set out with her until they reached Sadd ar-Rawhâ, where her menses ended, and he then married her. *Hais* (a kind of meal) was prepared and served on a small leather sheet. The Prophet (ﷺ) then said to me: Inform the others (about the wedding banquet).

This was the wedding banquet given by the Prophet (ﷺ) upon his marriage with Ṣafiyah (رضي الله عنها). Thereafter, we proceeded to Madinah, and I would see him covering her with his cloak, while she walked behind him. He would also kneel beside his camel, in order to let Ṣafiyah (رضي الله عنها) put her feet on his knees and climb on to the camel.»[47]

In the first of the above two hadiths, notice how the Prophet (ﷺ) came out of the mosque to see his wife home, even though he was in seclusion for the purpose of worship. On the part of the Prophet (ﷺ), this action shows that he had a great deal of respect and honour for his wife. He could easily have ended it by saying, "Go back home," but he did not do so; instead, through his good manners he tried to teach husbands how they should behave with their wives. We

---

[45] *Subḥân Allâh:* glory be to Allah

[46] Related by Bukhari

[47] Related by Bukhari

can appreciate this even more, if we know that all of the Prophet's wives lived in his house, except Ṣafiyah. The Prophet (ﷺ) had rented 'Usâmah's house for her, because he (ﷺ) had married her much later and there was no place in his own home where he could house her.

The second hadith shows even more courtesy and chivalry on the part of the Prophet Muhammad (ﷺ). He got down on his knees, and let his wife Ṣafiyah (رضي الله عنها) climb up on his knees in order to mount the camel. There is so much of respect and consideration in this action of his. Some cultures are proud that their men are gallant and chivalrous with women, and a man opens the car door for a woman, but look how our beloved Prophet (ﷺ) got down on his knees, in order to help his wife climb onto her camel. Surely, there can be no greater show of chivalry and respect.

Our beloved Prophet (ﷺ) has taught humankind the foundations of respect and good manners, which are to be applied not just with human beings, but with animals too.

It is honourable and cultured people who show respect and consideration for others. This is why Allah (عز وجل) has also ordered us to be respectful:

﴿مَّا لَكُمْ لَا تَرْجُونَ لِلَّهِ وَقَارًا ﴿١٣﴾ وَقَدْ خَلَقَكُمْ أَطْوَارًا ﴿١٤﴾﴾ [نوح: ١٣-١٤]

﴾What is [the matter] with you that you do not attribute to Allah [due] grandeur, while He has created you in stages?﴿ *(Qur'an 71: 13-14)*

Furthermore, the Prophet (ﷺ) has advised us to be considerate with the young and to honour our elders:

«The Prophet (ﷺ) said: Those who do not show mercy to our young ones, and do not respect the rights of our elders are not from amongst us.»[48]

---

[48] Ahmad, hadith no. 2196, authenticated by Shaykh al-Albâni

CHAPTER EIGHT
He was devoted to his wives

The Prophet's loyalty and devotion to his wives can be witnessed through the following hadiths:

«'Â'ishah (رضي الله عنها) narrated that whenever the Prophet (ﷺ) slaughtered a sheep, he would send some portions to Khadeejah's friends, saying: Send this to Khadeejah's friends. When I asked him about it one day, he said: Indeed I was nourished by her love.»[1]

'Â'ishah (رضي الله عنها) narrated another hadith: «An old woman came to the Prophet (ﷺ) while he was with me. He asked her: Who are you? She replied, I am Jassamah Mâziniyah. He said to her: In fact, you are Ḥassanah[2] Mâziniyah. How are you (all), how have you been doing? How did you fare after we left (Makkah)? She replied: Very well; may my mother and father be sacrificed for you, O Messenger of Allah! When she left, I said: You welcomed that old woman with such warmth? He replied: She used to visit us during Khadeejah's time, and it was certainly a beautiful era of faith.»[3]

«'Â'ishah (رضي الله عنها) said: Khadeejah's sister (Hâlah bint Khuwaylid) sought permission to enter the Prophet's rooms. It reminded him of how Khadeejah would seek permission, and he was overcome with grief, and said: O Allah! Hâlah bint Khuwaylid! This

---

[1] Muslim, hadith no. 6231

[2] 'A good deed' — the Prophet (ﷺ) was playing on the sound of her name in a nice way. (Editor)

[3] Al-Ḥâkim, *Al-Mustadrak*, hadith no. 41, 1/61; a sound narration

made me feel jealous, so I said: What do you miss so much about an old woman of Quraysh, one who had red jaws.[4] She perished with time, and Allah has replaced her for you with something better.»[5]

The hadiths above tell us about the importance of loyalty and devotion in a marital relationship in particular, and in other social relationships on a general level. Our beloved Prophet (ﷺ) has taught us how to be loyal and devoted to our wives and in all our relationships. The Arabic word *wafâ'*, which is translated here as 'loyalty and devotion', is a word steeped with meanings of perfection and completion, as we can see from the Qur'anic verse where Allah has used this word to describe Prophet Ibrâheem (*Alayhi as-salâm* — Peace be upon him):

﴿وَإِبْرَٰهِيمَ ٱلَّذِى وَفَّىٰٓ ٣٧﴾ [النّجم: ٣٧]

﴿And [of] Abraham, who fulfilled his obligations.﴾ *(Qur'an 53: 37)*

Allah (ﷻ) has created his messengers to be true in their speech, their feelings, and their actions. This is what a poet has written about the concept of *wafâ'*:

When you say 'Yes' to something, complete the task,
For indeed 'Yes' is a mandatory debt which the free have to pay,
However, if you say 'No', then relax and leave it,
So that people don't call you a liar.[6]

---

[4] 'Â'ishah was insinuating that her teeth had fallen out, leaving only her red gums to be seen.

[5] Muslim, hadith no. 6235

[6] *Al-Mustaṭraf*, p. 285

Loyalty and devotion between the two spouses make one of the pillars that hold up a marriage, and on which the couple's happiness depends. Such devotion and loyalty should not only be maintained in the lifetime of both spouses, but also after the death of either of them. However, in our times, it is very rarely found in our social relationships.

CHAPTER NINE

He was always eager to guide and to help his wives to improve

«Juwayriyah narrated: The Prophet (ﷺ) came to me when I was performing my morning supplications, after which he went off to his own affairs. He returned by midday, and upon finding me in the same state, he asked me: Are you still sitting here (supplicating)? I said yes, so he said: Should I not teach you some words, which if you recited them, would outweigh and be worthier than all of what you have been reciting since morning? They are: Glory be to Allah and praise is due to Him according to the number of His creations, according to the pleasure of His Self, according to the weight of His Throne and according to the ink (used in recording) the words (for His Praise).»[1]

Similarly, there is another hadith narrated by Juwayriyah and collected by Bukhari:

«It is transmitted by Qatâdah, who heard from Abu Ayyoob, who narrates it from Juwayriyah: The Prophet (ﷺ) entered her apartment on a Friday, whilst she was fasting. He asked her: Did you fast yesterday? She said: No. Then he asked her: Do you intend to fast tomorrow? She said: No. He told her: Then break your fast.»[2]

---

[1] Muslim, hadith no. 6864

[2] Bukhari, hadith no. 1986

I shall make do with only two narrations here, but the Sunnah is full of hadiths which show how the Prophet (ﷺ) guided Juwayriyah towards Islam. In fact, the reflective readers of her biography will be astonished to hear the story of how her father accepted Islam.

When he found out that his daughter Juwayriyah had fallen in the hands of the Prophet (ﷺ), he chose some camels and brought them to the Prophet (ﷺ), in order to ransom his daughter with them. During his journey, he looked at his camels, and thought that he especially liked two of them, so he hid those two camels in a valley known as 'Aqeeq. Then he came upon the Prophet (ﷺ) and said: The believers have taken my daughter, so I have come to ransom her with this. The Prophet (ﷺ) replied to him: And what about those two camels which you have hidden in the valley of 'Aqeeq? Al-Ḥârith (Juwayriyah's father) exclaimed, saying: I bear witness that there is none worthy of worship other than Allah and that you are the Messenger of Allah, for by Allah, none but Allah Himself could have informed you of this. Thereafter, his two sons also accepted Islam and so did his tribe.[3]

Juwayriyah (رضي الله عنها) was always eager to learn about Islam. She was pious and loved Allah. She would keep herself absorbed in worship. In addition, her father was like her in his religiosity, and it was because of his influence and the way he accepted Islam, that his entire tribe also accepted Islam.

In fact, the love of Islam and piety was not something limited only to our Mother Juwayriyah (رضي الله عنها), but it was common to all the other Mothers of the Believers too. Those who study their biographies know that all the wives were eager to learn more about

---

[3] *Seerah Ibn Hishâm*, 4/526

their religion, to attain piety and closeness to Allah. All this was not because they had a lot of free time and did not have anything else to do, but because they had been taught at the hands of the Prophet (ﷺ) himself.

«'Â'ishah (رضي الله عنها) narrated: When the last ten days (of Ramadan) began, the Prophet (ﷺ) would tighten his waist-cloth. He would stay up through the night and wake up his family also.»[4]

In another narration, Umm Salamah related: «One night, the Prophet (ﷺ) woke up panic-stricken, and exclaimed: Glory be to Allah! How many sorrows has Allah sent down! How many trials Allah has sent down! Who will awake the inhabitants of the rooms?[5] One who is clothed in this world, may be naked in the Hereafter.»[6]

This is how the Prophet (ﷺ) would inculcate in his wives the love of Islam. He would support them in their worship of Allah and help them to obey Allah and to get closer to Him.

The Prophet's legacy to his Companions was also along the same lines. In his most eloquent way, he would often answer to questions about common worldly things by relating them to the hereafter:

In a hadith narrated by Thu'bân, «'Umar (رضي الله عنه) asked the Prophet (ﷺ): O Messenger of Allah, what kind of wealth should we seek? The Prophet (ﷺ) replied: You should seek a grateful heart, a tongue that remembers Allah, and a believing wife, who would steer you towards the affairs of the Hereafter.»[7]

---

4 Bukhari, hadith no. 2000

5 i.e. his wives, so that they may offer extra night prayers

6 At-Tirmidhi, hadith no. 2227

7 Ibn Mâjah, hadith no. 1505 & 1856; authenticated by Al-Albâni,

This hadith holds great depth and insight with regards to the advice it has in it, as 'Umar had actually asked about wealth (implying material wealth), but the beloved Prophet (ﷺ) answered him by saying:

1. a grateful heart,
2. a tongue that remembers Allah,
3. a believing wife.

The Prophet (ﷺ) did not say *dirhams*[8] here, which shows that true prosperity is to be wealthy in religion and religiosity, and true poverty is to be deficient in religion and religiosity.

---

[8] *dirham*: a silver coin; a unit of currency

CHAPTER TEN
The incident involving the slander against 'Â'ishah and its effect on him

The incident of the slander against 'Â'ishah was certainly a very painful part of the Prophet's personal life. It was one of the most agonizing experiences of his life. For one whole month, the Prophet's heart was in a state of uncertainty and anguish, and so was that of his beloved wife, 'Â'ishah. The hearts of Abu Bakr and his wife (Umm Roomân, 'Â'ishah's mother) were in pain, and that of Safwân ibn al-Mu'aṭṭal too. The doubt, anxiety, and hurt experienced by all those involved knew no end. This is because 'Â'ishah (رضي الله عنها), the daughter of Abu Bakr, was still a very young girl, being only seventeen years of age, and the most delicate of sensibilities is a quintessential characteristic of this age.

Here we have, our Prophet (ﷺ), who had to bear having filth heaped on the very sanctity of his household and its reputation, while people gossiped about his chaste wife for one whole month. Meanwhile, he remained unable to put an end to it all, until the ache in his heart rose to an unbearable level, and finally Allah sent down Qur'anic verses to absolve 'Â'ishah (رضي الله عنها) from all blame, and to re-establish her purity and truthfulness. The verses reaffirmed the purity of the eminent household of the Prophet (ﷺ), revealed the identities of the hypocrites who had spread this falsehood, and laid down principles for the Muslim society as well, showing them how to deal with an important issue of this nature.

So listen carefully to this authentic narration, which has been related to us by the daughter of the Truthful (Abu Bakr) herself:[1] «Whenever Allah's Messenger (ﷺ) intended to go on a journey, he would draw lots amongst his wives, and the one on whom lot fell would accompany him. Therefore, he drew lots amongst us, to decide who to take with him on one of his military campaigns. The lot fell to me, and so I proceeded with the Messenger of Allah (ﷺ). This was after Allah's order of veiling (for women) had already been revealed. I was carried (on the back of a camel) in my howdah and dismounted while still in it (whenever we came to a stop-over). In this way, we kept going, until Allah's Messenger (ﷺ) returned from battle.

When we approached the city of Madinah, he announced at night that it was time for departure. While the news of departure was being announced, I got up and went beyond the army camps, in order to answer the call of nature. As I returned to my riding animal, I touched my chest to find that my necklace (made of black and white Dhofari beads) was missing. So I returned to look for my necklace and my search detained me for some time. Meanwhile, the people who used to lift my howdah onto my camel came and lifted my empty howdah and put it onto the back of my camel, thinking that I was in it. In those days we women were light in weight and lean, since food was scarce; also, at that time I was still a young girl. The men, therefore, disregarded the lightness of the howdah while lifting and carrying it. They made the camel rise and all of them left. I found my necklace after the army had gone.

When I returned to the campsite, there was no caller to be found, nor anyone to listen to his call, so I decided to go to the place where I used to stay, thinking that they would miss me and come back looking for me. While I was sitting there, sleep overcame me and I slept. Ṣafwân ibn al-Mu'aṭṭal as-Sulamee adh-Dhakwânee had

---

[1] Muslim, hadith no. 6951

been positioned (as a guard) at the rear of the army. When he reached my place in the morning, he saw the figure of a sleeping person and recognized me instantly, because he had seen me before I started to veil myself. I woke up when he said out loud: *Innâ lillâhi wa innâ ilayhi râji'oon.*[2] I immediately veiled my face with my head cover, and by Allah, we did not speak a single word, and I did not hear him say anything other than *innâ lillâhi wa innâ ilayhi râji'oon.* He dismounted from his camel and made it kneel down, putting his leg on its front legs, and I mounted it. Then he set forth, leading the camel that was carrying me, until we overtook the army in the extreme heat of midday while they were taking a break. (Due to this incident) some people brought destruction upon themselves, and the one who forged this slander was 'Abdullâh ibn Ubay ibn Salool.

After we returned to Madinah, I fell seriously ill for a month. People were propagating the forged statements of the slanderers while I was completely unaware of it, but I did feel that during this particular illness, I was not receiving the same kindness from the Prophet (ﷺ) as I used to receive from him when I had been ill before. This time, Allah's Messenger (ﷺ) would only come, greet me and say: How is that (lady)? — and then leave. That aroused my suspicion, but I did not discover the evil (slander) till I went out after my convalescence, accompanied by Umm Misṭaḥ to the place where we used to answer the call of nature, because we would only go at night to do this. This was before we had latrines in our houses. This habit of ours was in conformity with the habit of the ancient Arabs living in the deserts,[3] for it would be troublesome for us to have our latrines near our houses.

---

[2] *innâ lillâhi wa innâ ilayhi râji'oon*: 'to Allah we belong and to Him is our return'; a phrase uttered during times of difficulty [from *Soorat al-Baqarah* (2: 156)]

[3] This was also the habit of the non-Arabs of that time.

So I went with Umm Misṭaḥ, who was the daughter of Abu Ruhm ibn al-Muṭṭalib ibn 'Abd Manâf, whose mother was the daughter of Sakhr ibn 'Âmir and the aunt of Abu Bakr aṣ-Ṣiddeeq and whose son was Misṭaḥ ibn Uthâthah ibn 'Abbâs ibn al-Muṭṭalib. Umm Misṭaḥ and I returned to my house after we finished answering the call of nature. Umm Misṭaḥ stumbled when her foot got entangled in her cloak, so she muttered: Let Misṭaḥ be ruined! I said: What a hard word you have said! How could you abuse a man who took part in the battle of Badr? On that she said: O you *hantâh*![4] Didn't you hear what he said? I asked: What did he say?

Then she told me about the slander that was being spread by a group of people. This aggravated my ailment, and when I reached my home, the Messenger of Allah (ﷺ) came to me, and after greeting me, said: How is that (lady)? I said: Will you allow me to go to my parents' house? I wanted to confirm the news from them. The Messenger of Allah (ﷺ) gave me his permission, so I went to my parents and asked my mother: Mother, what are people talking about? She said: O my daughter! Don't worry, for scarcely is there a charming woman who is loved by her husband and whose husband has other wives besides herself that (these women) would find fault with her. I said, Glory be to Allah! Are the people really talking in this way? I wept through that entire night, and when dawn broke, I could neither stop weeping nor could I sleep. That whole morning, I kept on weeping.

When the divine inspiration was delayed, Allah's Messenger (ﷺ) called 'Ali ibn Abi Ṭâlib and Usâmah ibn Zayd to seek their advice. 'Usâmah ibn Zayd talked about what he knew of my innocence, and the respect he preserved in himself for me. 'Usâmah

---

[4] *hantâh*: a word used to address one who is far away, but may also be used for one who is near

said: O Messenger of Allah! She is your wife and we do not know anything except good about her. 'Ali ibn Abi Ṭâlib (رضي الله عنه) said: O Messenger of Allah! Allah does not put you in difficulty; there are plenty of women other than her. However, ask the maidservant, who can tell you the truth. So Allah's Messenger (ﷺ) called Bareerah (the maidservant) and said: Bareerah, did you ever see anything about 'Â'ishah that may have aroused your suspicion? Bareerah replied: By Him Who has sent you with the Truth, I have never seen anything in her for which I might blame her, except that she is a very young girl who falls asleep whilst her family's dough lies uncovered, and the domestic goats come and eat it.

Hence, the Messenger of Allah (ﷺ) ascended the pulpit and complained about 'Abdullâh ibn Ubay (ibn Salool) in front of his Companions. He said: O community of Muslims! Who will relieve me from the pain which that man has inflicted upon me, by saying such an evil thing about my family? By Allah, I have known nothing but good from my family and they have blamed a man about whom I have known nothing except good. He would never enter my home except in my company. Sa'd ibn Mu'âdh got up and said: O Messenger of Allah! I will relieve you from him. If he is from the tribe of Al-Aws, I will chop his head off, and if he is from our tribe of Al-Khazraj, then give us your command, and we will fulfil it. Upon this, a man from Al-Khazraj got up. He was Sa'd ibn 'Ubâdah, chief of Al-Khazraj. He was a pious man, but his love for his tribe goaded him into saying to Sa'd (ibn Mu'âdh): By Allah, you have told a lie; you shall not and cannot kill him. If he belonged to your people, you would not wish him to be killed.

Upon this, Usayd ibn Ḥuḍayr, who was the cousin of Sa'd (ibn Mu'âdh) got up and said to Sa'd ibn 'Ubâdah: By Allah! You are a liar! We will surely kill him, and you are a hypocrite arguing on the behalf of hypocrites. On this, the two tribes of Al-Aws and Al

Khazraj got so excited that they were about to start fighting, whilst the Prophet (ﷺ) was still standing on the pulpit. Allah's Messenger (ﷺ) quieted them down until they became silent, and he was silent, too.

All that day, I kept weeping, with my tears never ceasing and no sleep touching my eyes. For the next two nights, I kept on weeping, and did not sleep at all, until my parents thought that my liver would burst because of so much crying. Thus, while my parents were sitting with me and I was weeping, an Anṣâri woman came and sought permission to enter. I granted her permission, she came in, sat down and started weeping too. While we were in this state, the Messenger of Allah (ﷺ) came, greeted us and sat down. He had not sat with me since the day that what was being said about me had been uttered. A month had elapsed and no divine inspiration had come to him concerning my case. The Messenger of Allah (ﷺ) recited the *tashahhud*[5] and then said: O 'Â'ishah, I have been told some things about you. If you are innocent, Allah will soon reveal your innocence, and if you have committed a sin, repent to Allah and seek His forgiveness, for when a slave confesses his sins and seeks Allah's forgiveness, Allah accepts his repentance.

When the Messenger of Allah (ﷺ) finished his speech, my tears finally ceased flowing, and I could no longer feel a single drop. I said to my father: Reply to the Prophet (ﷺ) on my behalf, concerning what he has said. My father said: By Allah, I do not know what to say to Allah's Messenger (ﷺ). Then I said to my mother: Reply to Allah's Messenger (ﷺ) on my behalf, concerning what he has said. She said: By Allah, I do not know what to say to the Messenger of Allah (ﷺ). In spite of the fact that I was still a young girl and had

---

[5] *tashahhud*: the testimony that states that there is none worthy of worship other than Allah, He has no partners, and that Muhammad (ﷺ) is His Slave and His Messenger

little knowledge of the Qur'an, I said: By Allah, I certainly know that you have heard this (slanderous) speech and that it has been planted in your hearts (and minds) and you have taken it as the truth. Now, if I tell you that I am innocent — and Allah knows that I am innocent — you will not believe me; and if I confess to be guilty — and Allah knows that I am innocent — you will believe me. By Allah, I can find no similitude for me and you, except that of Joseph's father when he said:

﴿... فَصَبْرٌ جَمِيلٌ وَٱللَّهُ ٱلْمُسْتَعَانُ عَلَىٰ مَا تَصِفُونَ ﴿١٨﴾﴾ [يوسف: ١٨]

﴿... So [for me] patience is most fitting against that which you assert; it is Allah [Alone] Whose Help can be sought.﴾ (*Qur'an 12: 18*)

Then I turned away and lay on my bed. Allah knew that I was innocent and I hoped that Allah would reveal my innocence. However, by Allah, I never thought that Allah would reveal for my sake, verses which would be recited (forever). I considered myself too unworthy to be mentioned by Allah, so I hoped that His Messenger (ﷺ) might have a dream or a vision in which Allah would prove my innocence. However, by Allah, before the Messenger (ﷺ) even left his seat, and before any of the household left their places, Allah revealed divine inspiration to His Messenger (ﷺ).

Then, the same difficult condition overtook him, which used to overtake him (whenever he used to be divinely inspired). He became feverish, and sweat was dripping from his body like pearls, although it was a wintry day. This was because of the weight of the statement that was being revealed to him by Allah. When Allah's Messenger (ﷺ) got over this state of his, he got up smiling, and the first words he uttered were: O 'Â'ishah! Allah has declared your innocence! My mother said to me: Get up and go to him. I replied: By Allah, I will not go to him. I praise none but Allah; He is the one who has revealed my innocence. Allah revealed these verses to absolve me of all blame: ﴿Indeed, those who came with falsehood are a group among you...﴾ (24: 11-20)»

﴿إِنَّ ٱلَّذِينَ جَآءُو بِٱلۡإِفۡكِ عُصۡبَةٌ مِّنكُمۡۚ لَا تَحۡسَبُوهُ شَرًّا لَّكُمۖ بَلۡ هُوَ خَيۡرٌ لَّكُمۡۚ لِكُلِّ
ٱمۡرِيٍٕ مِّنۡهُم مَّا ٱكۡتَسَبَ مِنَ ٱلۡإِثۡمِۚ وَٱلَّذِي تَوَلَّىٰ كِبۡرَهُۥ مِنۡهُمۡ لَهُۥ عَذَابٌ عَظِيمٌ ﴿١١﴾
لَّوۡلَآ إِذۡ سَمِعۡتُمُوهُ ظَنَّ ٱلۡمُؤۡمِنُونَ وَٱلۡمُؤۡمِنَٰتُ بِأَنفُسِهِمۡ خَيۡرًا وَقَالُواْ هَٰذَآ إِفۡكٌ
مُّبِينٌ ﴿١٢﴾ لَّوۡلَا جَآءُو عَلَيۡهِ بِأَرۡبَعَةِ شُهَدَآءَۚ فَإِذۡ لَمۡ يَأۡتُواْ بِٱلشُّهَدَآءِ فَأُوْلَٰٓئِكَ عِندَ
ٱللَّهِ هُمُ ٱلۡكَٰذِبُونَ ﴿١٣﴾ وَلَوۡلَا فَضۡلُ ٱللَّهِ عَلَيۡكُمۡ وَرَحۡمَتُهُۥ فِي ٱلدُّنۡيَا وَٱلۡأٓخِرَةِ لَمَسَّكُمۡ
فِي مَآ أَفَضۡتُمۡ فِيهِ عَذَابٌ عَظِيمٌ ﴿١٤﴾ إِذۡ تَلَقَّوۡنَهُۥ بِأَلۡسِنَتِكُمۡ وَتَقُولُونَ بِأَفۡوَاهِكُم مَّا
لَيۡسَ لَكُم بِهِۦ عِلۡمٌ وَتَحۡسَبُونَهُۥ هَيِّنًا وَهُوَ عِندَ ٱللَّهِ عَظِيمٌ ﴿١٥﴾ وَلَوۡلَآ إِذۡ سَمِعۡتُمُوهُ
قُلۡتُم مَّا يَكُونُ لَنَآ أَن نَّتَكَلَّمَ بِهَٰذَا سُبۡحَٰنَكَ هَٰذَا بُهۡتَٰنٌ عَظِيمٌ ﴿١٦﴾ يَعِظُكُمُ ٱللَّهُ أَن
تَعُودُواْ لِمِثۡلِهِۦٓ أَبَدًا إِن كُنتُم مُّؤۡمِنِينَ ﴿١٧﴾ وَيُبَيِّنُ ٱللَّهُ لَكُمُ ٱلۡأٓيَٰتِۚ وَٱللَّهُ عَلِيمٌ
حَكِيمٌ ﴿١٨﴾ إِنَّ ٱلَّذِينَ يُحِبُّونَ أَن تَشِيعَ ٱلۡفَٰحِشَةُ فِي ٱلَّذِينَ ءَامَنُواْ لَهُمۡ عَذَابٌ
أَلِيمٌ فِي ٱلدُّنۡيَا وَٱلۡأٓخِرَةِۚ وَٱللَّهُ يَعۡلَمُ وَأَنتُمۡ لَا تَعۡلَمُونَ ﴿١٩﴾ وَلَوۡلَا فَضۡلُ ٱللَّهِ
عَلَيۡكُمۡ وَرَحۡمَتُهُۥ وَأَنَّ ٱللَّهَ رَءُوفٌ رَّحِيمٌ ﴿٢٠﴾﴾ [النور: ١١-٢٠]

﴿Indeed, those who came with falsehood are a group among you. Do not think it bad for you; rather it is good for you. For every person among them is what [punishment] he has earned from the sin, and he who took upon himself the greater portion thereof-for him is a great punishment. Why, when you heard it, did not the believing men and believing women think good of one another and say: This is an obvious falsehood. Why did they [who slandered] not produce for it four witnesses? And when they do not produce the witnesses, then it is they, in the sight of Allah, who are the liars. And if it had not been for the favour of Allah upon you and His mercy in this world and the Hereafter, you would have been touched for that [lie] in which you were involved by a great punishment. When you received it with your tongues and said with your mouths that of which you had no knowledge and thought it was insignificant while it was, in the sight of Allah, tremendous. And why, when you heard it, did you not say: It is not for us to speak of this. Exalted are You, [O Allah]; this is a great slander. Allah warns you against returning to the likes of this [conduct], ever, if you should be believers. And Allah makes clear to you the verses, and Allah is Knowing and Wise. Indeed, those who like that immorality should be spread [or publicized] among those who have believed will have a painful punishment in this world and the Hereafter. And Allah knows and you do not know. And if it had not been for the favour of Allah upon you and His mercy — and because Allah is Kind and Merciful [you would have all been punished].﴿ *(Qur'an 24: 11-20)*

This incident contained exhortation for the Prophet's heart. It taught him a lesson and provided him with solace. We can feel the effect it must have had upon all of them, and we can see how it especially affected the Prophet (ﷺ), and how Allah sent down definitive Qur'anic verses, all the way from above the seven heavens, in order to clear 'Â'ishah's name.[6]

Following are some of the lessons that may be learnt from this hadith:[7]

❖ It is allowed for a man to travel with his wife.

❖ Men are allowed to serve women on such journeys.

❖ If a man is not a *maḥram*[8] of the woman, and he helps her climb

---

[6] *Sharḥ Muslim* by An-Nawawi (17/ 261-264)

[7] *Sharḥ Muslim* by An-Nawawi (17/ 261-264)

[8] *maḥram*: a degree of consanguinity precluding marriage; a man whom a woman may never marry due to the close blood or marriage relationship. e.g., father, brother, son, uncle, and father-in-law

onto her camel or into her vehicle, then he should not speak to her, unless it is necessary to do so. This can be deduced from the fact that the men who carried the howdah never addressed the woman they thought was in the howdah.

❖ A woman should veil herself from the gaze of strangers who are male, even though they may be pious and God-fearing.

❖ It is commendable for a husband to be kind and indulgent with his wife, living with her in an amiable fashion.

❖ The wife should not go to her parents' house without her husband's permission.

❖ It is recommended for a person to seek advice from his or her advisors, family, and friends.

❖ It absolved 'Â'ishah (رضي الله عنها) from all that she was accused of through this false rumour, and this exoneration was established through the verses of the Qur'an itself, which makes it most definitive and authoritative. Consequently, if any human being now doubts her, Allah forbid, he or she will become a non-believer, apostatising from the community of Muslims. Ibn 'Abbâs and others have said:

> None of the wives of any of the Prophets (May Allah send blessings and peace upon all of them) has ever engaged in illicit sexual relations, and this is an honour that Allah, the Almighty, has granted all of them.

PART THREE
Doubts Regarding the Prophet (ﷺ)

This section consists of one chapter:

Chapter Eleven: Plural marriages

CHAPTER ELEVEN
Plural marriages

It states in the Torah that the Prophet Solomon (or Sulaymân, as he is called in Arabic) had 700 concubines and 300 wives[1] and Prophet Abraham (Ibrâheem) had two wives Sarah and Hagar (Hâjar). Furthermore, the Bible does not prohibit polygyny either, as Jesus (Eesâ) came to complete the message brought forth in the law of Moses (Moosâ), as Allah (ﷻ) says:

﴿وَإِذْ قَالَ عِيسَى ٱبْنُ مَرْيَمَ يَٰبَنِىٓ إِسْرَٰٓءِيلَ إِنِّى رَسُولُ ٱللَّهِ إِلَيْكُم مُّصَدِّقًا لِّمَا بَيْنَ يَدَىَّ مِنَ ٱلتَّوْرَىٰةِ وَمُبَشِّرًۢا بِرَسُولٍ يَأْتِى مِنۢ بَعْدِى ٱسْمُهُۥٓ أَحْمَدُ ۖ فَلَمَّا جَآءَهُم بِٱلْبَيِّنَٰتِ قَالُوا۟ هَٰذَا سِحْرٌ مُّبِينٌ ۝٦﴾ [الصَّف: ٦]

﴾And [mention] when Jesus, the son of Mary, said: O children of Israel, indeed I am the messenger of Allah to you, confirming what came before me of the Torah and bringing good tidings of a messenger to come after me, whose name is Ahmad. But when he came to them with clear evidence, they said: This is obvious magic.﴿ *(Qur'an 61: 6)*

Hence, plural marriages were common and widespread amongst the Arabs before Islam. We have the example of Ghaylân ibn Salamah ath-Thaqafee, who was married to ten women in the days of ignorance. When he accepted Islam, all his wives accepted

---

[1] *Al-Mar'ah bayn al-Fiqh wal-Qânoon*, p. 71

Islam with him, and the Prophet (ﷺ) ordered him to choose only four from amongst them, and divorce the rest.[2]

This shows us that polygyny was not something unheard of that Islam had introduced into the world. There are many who use this issue to speak in error about Islam and the Muslims, waging an intellectual war against this religion, by disguising the truth and even vilifying the virtuous personality of the Prophet (ﷺ), because of his plural marriages. They unjustly accuse him of being sexually driven, having strong carnal desires, and seeking only his personal pleasure through these marriages. In this way, they totally twist the truth, and this is a common practice amongst Jewish and Christian Orientalists. Unfortunately, there are many people from amongst our own ranks, who applaud them for saying that polygyny is a 'dire insult to women'.[3]

We say to those people, whose thinking has been corrupted by the Christian missionary onslaught, that polygyny is a blessing from Allah, and that there is great wisdom behind it, which we may not have fully understood, had we not the example of the Prophet (ﷺ) in front of us. In addition, his plural marriages also served as a means of propagating Islam.

Let us go back and look at the words of Allah:

﴿وَإِنْ خِفْتُمْ أَلَّا تُقْسِطُوا۟ فِى ٱلْيَتَٰمَىٰ فَٱنكِحُوا۟ مَا طَابَ لَكُم مِّنَ ٱلنِّسَآءِ مَثْنَىٰ وَثُلَٰثَ وَرُبَٰعَ ۖ فَإِنْ خِفْتُمْ أَلَّا تَعْدِلُوا۟ فَوَٰحِدَةً أَوْ مَا مَلَكَتْ أَيْمَٰنُكُمْ ۚ ذَٰلِكَ أَدْنَىٰٓ أَلَّا تَعُولُوا۟ ﴿٣﴾﴾

[النِّسَاء : ٣]

﴾If you fear that you shall not be able to deal justly with the orphans,

[2] Ibn Mâjah, hadith no. 1983. Al-Albâni termed it *ḥasan*, 2/350; a sound narration, as it is recorded in *Irwâ al-Ghaleel,* hadith no. 1885

[3] *Limâdha al-Ḥujoom 'alâ ta'addud az-Zawjât*, p. 35

marry women of your choice, two, or three, or four; but if you fear that you shall not be able to deal justly [with them], then only one, or [captives] that your right hands possess. That will be more suitable, to prevent you from doing injustice.﴿ *(Qur'an 4: 3)*

Ibn Katheer (may Allah have mercy upon him) says: "The word *'awl*[4] here means injustice."[5] This means that to suffice with just one wife is the best way to avoid falling into any kind of injustice and oppression.

Allah (ﷻ) says:

﴿وَلَن تَسْتَطِيعُوٓا۟ أَن تَعْدِلُوا۟ بَيْنَ ٱلنِّسَآءِ وَلَوْ حَرَصْتُمْ ۖ فَلَا تَمِيلُوا۟ كُلَّ ٱلْمَيْلِ فَتَذَرُوهَا كَٱلْمُعَلَّقَةِ ۚ وَإِن تُصْلِحُوا۟ وَتَتَّقُوا۟ فَإِنَّ ٱللَّهَ كَانَ غَفُورًا رَّحِيمًا ﴿١٢٩﴾﴾ [النِّساء: ١٢٩]

﴾You will never be able to deal perfectly justly between your wives even if it is your ardent desire, so do not incline too much toward one of them [by giving her more of your time and provision] so as to leave the other hanging [neither divorced nor yet truly married]. And if you do right, and fear Allah, then Allah is Oft-Forgiving, Most Merciful.﴿[6] *(Qur'an 4: 129)*

Three issues are raised in this verse:

First: Islam has not made the practice of polygyny mandatory; in fact, it mentions it in a way that shows that it often leads people into being oppressive and unjust.

---

[4] i.e., the root of the verb *ta'ooloo*, which is the form in this verse (Editor)

[5] *Tafseer al-Qur'an al-'Adheem*, (1/589)

[6] This interpretation is adapted from that of M. Taqi-ud-Deen al-Hilâli and M. Muḥsin Khân, in their Interpretation of the Meanings of the Noble Qur'an in the English Language, Riyadh: Maktaba Dar-us-Salam, 1993. (Translator)

Second: Neither has Islam completely forbidden the practice, but it takes into consideration the fact that it is the nature of many men to desire more than one woman. Also, sometimes men marry again in the quest of offspring, which they may not be able to get from a barren wife. Moreover, some men may be wealthier than others and may like to spend their money in supporting another woman.

Third: Even though Islam permits plural marriage, it lays down certain principles, exhorting people to be just, as has already been mentioned, which makes people take polygyny more seriously.[7]

Scholars have given various reasons to explain the wisdom behind polygyny, some of which have been mentioned here:

1. Acquiring offspring: There are hadiths which show that the Prophet (ﷺ) was proud of his Ummah for having many children.

2. Women outnumbering men:[8]

«Abu Moosâ al-Ash'ari reports that the Prophet (ﷺ) said: It will come to pass[9] that a single man may have forty women as his dependants, as there will be many women and few men.»[10]

3. Men are different in nature from women: This is in terms of their physical make-up, where men remain reproductive until seventy years of age or more, whereas most women become unable to bear children after the age of fifty. Hence, a man may still want to father children even after his first wife can no longer conceive.

---

[7] *Al-Hayât az-Zawjiyyah min Mindhâr ash-Sharee'ah al-Islâmiyah*, p.150

[8] It is a verifiable fact that modern census data show that the number of women exceeds that of men in most parts of the world, except in regions where female infanticide is still practiced, in which case the ratios are reversed. (Editor)

[9] This hadith is in reference to the signs of the approach of Judgment Day. (Editor)

[10] Bukhari, Book of Zakât, hadith no. 1414

4. The illness of a wife: In a situation in which the wife is terminally or chronically ill, the husband has two choices, either to bring a co-wife into the family or to divorce his sick wife. Since divorce often leads to great social and financial difficulty for the woman and her children, we believe that polygamy is a better option for all concerned.

5. Infertility: Sometimes, the wife is sterile but the husband desires to have children, and here too, the best option is a second marriage.

6. Continuous travelling: Some men are always travelling or are forced to live away from their wives (in foreign countries), and they may have children from the first wife, but are unable to satisfy their desires while away from her for so long. For such men, it is better and more chaste to marry another woman, than to become involved in illicit relationships.[11]

As for our Prophet (ﷺ), we have seen that his plural marriages were a means of spreading the message of Islam. He did not marry these women to fulfil his sexual desires; if this were true, why did Allah then forbid him from divorcing any of them or to marry other women? If he wanted to just follow his own whims and desires, why did he not marry anyone other than Khadeejah (رضي الله عنها) before Islam? Moreover, he spent almost all his youth with her, as we know that he was married to her for twenty-five years.[12] Furthermore, none of the women he married was a virgin, except 'Â'ishah (رضي الله عنها), and in spite of this, the Prophet (ﷺ) was a loyal and faithful husband to all of them.

Apart from this, his duty of spreading the message of Islam required him to have strong conjugal ties with persons of authority in the tribes of his region. This is why he married into families from the Quraysh tribe, as well as other tribes of significance, like those of the

---

[11] *Ishrat an-Nisâ'*, p. 136

[12] *Ar-Raḥeeq al-Makhtoom*, p. 57

Jews. Another reason for marrying so many women was to teach the Ummah how to treat women, and in this way, the Prophet (ﷺ) became the best of mentors (in marital affairs), through his words and actions.

The Prophet (ﷺ) gave the severest warning for a person who had more than one wife and did not treat them equally, for he said: «He who had two wives and was inclined towards one of them, (ignoring) the other one, will be (raised on the Day of Judgment) with one half of his body missing.»[13]

It has been narrated that some of the pious predecessors in Islamic history were so cautious about this, that if they had two wives, they would try to treat them equally with regards to kisses too, in fact some of them would perfume themselves alternately between the two wives' houses. Ibn Seereen mentions that he did not even like to perform his ablutions in the house of one wife, and not in the other wife's, (because the latter may feel unjustly treated). Such a perfect sense of equality is what Allah loves.

Imam Al-Ghazâli writes in his book *Ihyâ' 'Uloom ad-Deen*:[14] If a man has more than one wife, it is obligatory on him to be just with them, without being inclined towards any one of them. If he travels, and seeks the company of one of his wives during this journey, he should draw lots for which one of his wives should accompany him, as the Prophet (ﷺ) used to do.[15] Moreover, if it so happens that a wife misses her right to a night with him, then the husband should make up for it by spending an extra night with her, and this compensation is obligatory for him.

---

[13] Ibn Mâjah, hadith no. 2000; graded as a sound narration by Al-Albâni, in *Irwâ' al-Ghaleel*

[14] *Ihyâ' Uloom ad-Deen*, (504)

[15] Bukhari, hadith no. 5211

Hence, the husband should also be fair with how much pocket money he gives to each and how many nights he spends with each of them. As for love and sexual intercourse, that is something beyond his control, which is why Allah (ﷻ) says in the Qur'an:

﴿وَلَن تَسْتَطِيعُوٓاْ أَن تَعْدِلُواْ بَيْنَ ٱلنِّسَآءِ وَلَوْ حَرَصْتُمْ ۖ فَلَا تَمِيلُواْ كُلَّ ٱلْمَيْلِ فَتَذَرُوهَا كَٱلْمُعَلَّقَةِ ۚ وَإِن تُصْلِحُواْ وَتَتَّقُواْ فَإِنَّ ٱللَّهَ كَانَ غَفُورًا رَّحِيمًا ﴿١٢٩﴾﴾ [النِّساء: ١٢٩]

﴿You will never be able to deal perfectly justly between your wives even if it is your ardent desire, so do not incline too much toward one of them [by giving her more of your time and provision] so as to leave the other hanging [neither divorced nor yet truly married]. And if you do right, and fear Allah, then Allah is Oft-Forgiving, Most Merciful.﴾ *(Qur'an 4: 129)*

This refers to being just with regards to one's sexual desire and the inclination of one's heart, and this is where inequality and injustice will take place.[16] The Prophet (ﷺ) would treat his wives equally with regards to how much money he gave them or how many nights he spent with them, but even he said: «O Allah! I struggle to be fair regarding that which I possess. However, I do not have any control over that which you possess, and I do not (that is, my heart).»[17]

May my father and my mother be sacrificed for you, O Muhammad!

---

[16] *Fatḥ ul-Qadeer*, (1/680)

[17] Tirmidhi, hadith no. 11406, 4/325, termed as weak by Al-Albâni in *Al-Irwâ' al-Ghaleel,* (2018) and *At-Targheeb wa at-Tarheeb,* (3/79). One version of the hadith has been graded as sound by Ibn Ḥibbân and Al-Ḥâkim.

The marriages of the Prophet (bpuh)

Name	Marital situation (at the time of marriage to the Prophet (bpuh))	Age at which she married the Prophet (bpuh)	Age of the Prophet (bpuh) at the time he married her	The circumstances in which the marriage took place
Khadeejah bint Khwailid	The widow of Abu Hâlah at-Tameemee and then of 'Ateeq al-Makhzoomee (with whom she had 4 children).	40 years	25 years	She was the one who proposed marriage to him, so he accepted the proposal because he saw that she was a distinguished woman of high morals and good character.
Sawdah bint Zam'ah	The widow of Sakrân ibn 'Amru (with whom she had 5 children).	55 years	50 years	She was from amongst the believing emigrants, and the Prophet (bpuh) feared that she would be tortured by her family if he sent her back.
'Â'ishah bint Abu Bakr	Unmarried	9 years	53 years	He married her in order to strengthen his relationship with his best friend, and also to demolish the custom of Arabs in which men did not marry into families of people with whom they were very close friends, as they considered them to be like blood relations.
Ḥafṣah bint 'Umar	The widow of Khunays ibn Ḥudhâfah	19 years	55 years	He married her to gratify 'Umar ibn Al-Khattâb and to strengthen his relationship with him
Zaynab bint Khuzaymah	The widow of 'Ubaydah ibn Al-Ḥârith and the divorcee of Ṭufail ibn Al-Ḥârith	60 years	56 years	Her husband had been martyred in the battle of Badr. She was a persevering believer who had spent everything she had for the sake of Islam, and the Prophet (bpuh) liked her for this.
Hind bint Abee 'Umayyah	The widow of Abdullah ibn Al-Asad (with whom	65 years	57 years	She was a mother to 4 orphans and her husband had been martyred, so the

The marriages of the Prophet (bpuh)

(Umm Salamah)	she had 4 children).			Prophet (bpuh) desired to take their charge.
Zaynab bint Jaḥsh	She was the divorcee of Zayd ibn Ḥârithah	25 years	58 years	Allah ordered the Prophet (bpuh) to marry her, in order to negate the custom of treating adopted children as biological children.
Juwayriyah bint Al-Ḥârith	The widow of Musâfi‘ ibn Ṣafwân	20 years	59 years	She was the daughter of the chief of Banu Muṣṭaliq, and because of this marriage, her father released the prisoners taken during the battle of Bani Muṣṭaliq, and he and his tribe accepted Islam.
Umm Ḥabeebah bint Abee Sufyân	The widow of ‘Ubaid Allah ibn Jaḥsh	40 years	59 years	When her first husband apostatised, she was in Abyssinia. She did not have anyone to support her there, so the Prophet (bpuh) married her, with King Negus as a witness to this marriage.
Ṣafiyah bint Ḥuyay	The widow of Salâm ibn Mashkam and Kinânah ibn Ar-Rabee‘	17 years	59 years	She was one of the captives from the victorious battle of Khaybar, and the Prophet (bpuh) freed her and married her.
Maymoonah bint Al-Ḥârith	The widow of Abu Rahm ibn ‘Abdul ‘Uzzah and the divorcee of Mas‘ood ibn ‘Amru Ath-Thaqafee	26 years	61 years	The Prophet’s goal was to increase unity amongst the Arab tribes and the reason for this marriage was to bring the tribes of Banu Hâshim and Banu Makhzoom closer together.

The descendants of Muhammad ibn ‘Abdullâh (s) (page 1/2)

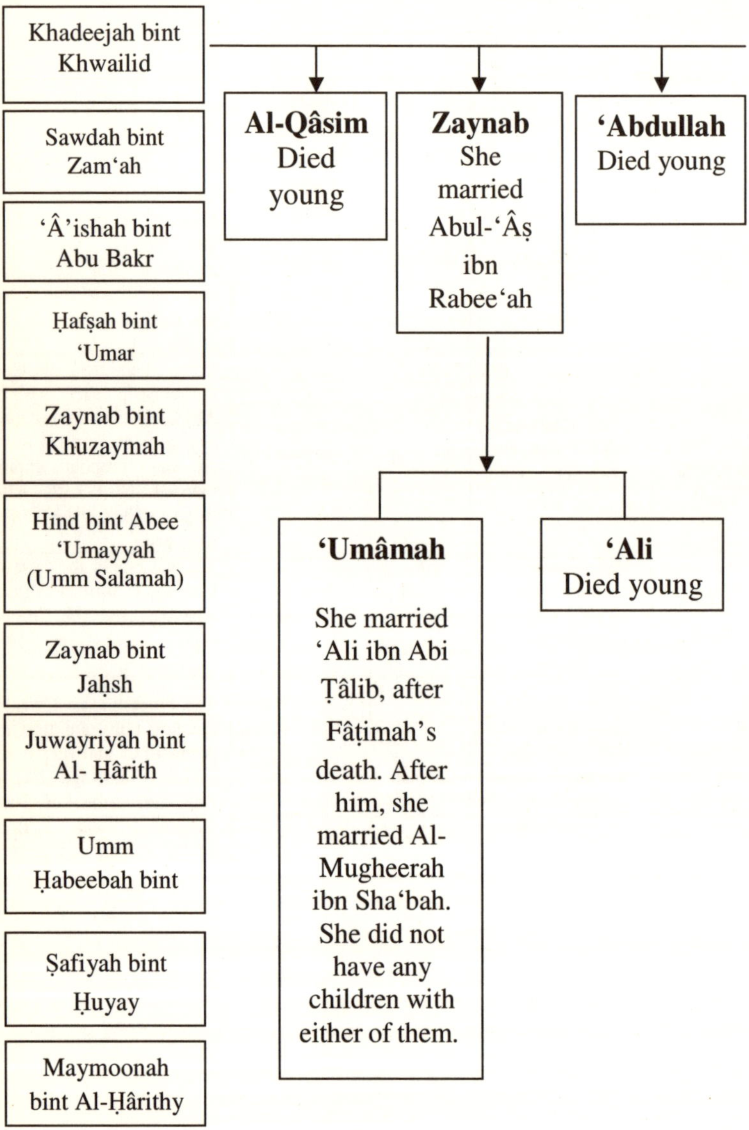

The descendants of Muhammad ibn 'Abdullâh (s) (page 2/2)

Khadeejah bint Khwailid

Ruqayyah	**Umm Kulthum**	**Fâṭimah**
She married 'Utbah ibn Abi Lahab, who divorced her before consummating the marriage, after which she married 'Uthmân ibn 'Affân. They had a baby boy, 'Abdullah, who died young.	She married 'Utaibah ibn Abu Lahab, who divorced her before consummating the marriage, after which she married 'Uthmân ibn 'Affân when he had become a widower after Ruqayyah's death. She never had any children with him.	She married 'Ali ibn Abi Ṭâlib, and had four children with him.

Children of Fâṭimah:

Al-Ḥasan	**Al-Ḥusayn**	**Zaynab**	**Umm Kulthum**
He had eleven children: 'Abdullah, Qâsim, Ḥasan, Zayd, 'Amru, 'Ubaidullah, Abdur-Raḥmân, Aḥmad, Ismâ'eel, Ḥusayn, 'Aqeel, and Umm Ḥasan.	He had nine children: 'Ali Akbar, 'Ali Zayn Al-'Âbideen, 'Ali Aṣghar, Muhammad, 'Abdullah, Ja'far, Zaynab, Sukaynah and Fâṭimah.	She married 'Abdullah ibn Ja'far, and had three children with him: Ali, 'Awn, and Umm Kulthum.	She married 'Umar ibn Al-Khaṭṭâb and had two children with him, Zayd and Ruqayyah.

In Conclusion

All praises are for Allah, by whose blessings all good deeds are accomplished, and who has helped me to complete this book, my humble offering: *Prophet Muhammad (ﷺ): the best of all husbands.* I hope that this book serves as a source of enlightenment and a worthy addition to homes around the world. My deepest thanks and acknowledgements go to my brothers in Islam, the men at the Family Development Centre in *Al-Hasa*, for their blessed efforts at serving their Prophet (ﷺ) — as well as others — in this regard. The Messenger's role as a husband is only a small aspect of what he has done for our great religion, Islam. I implore my brothers and sisters in faith to be kind and gentle whilst calling people towards this religion, by giving them an insight into the Sunnah of the Prophet (ﷺ). Surely, the seed of goodness lies within their hearts, but the burning question is: how can it be allowed to germinate, so as to allow people to recognize it within themselves?

May blessings and peace be upon our Prophet Muhammad.

All praises are for Allah, the Lord of all worlds.

Glossary of Islamic terms[1]

Anṣâr	أنصار	'helpers': the Muslim citizens of Madinah who gave refuge to the Prophet (ﷺ) and the other Muslim emigrants from Makkah
dirham	درهم	a silver coin; a unit of currency
fiṭrah	فطرة	the natural inclination (of humans) instilled by Allah
hadith (ḥadeeth)	حديث	a saying or action of Prophet Muhammad (ﷺ) that was remembered and recorded by his Companions and followers
hantâh	هنتاه	a word used to address one who is far away, but may also be used for one who is near
iḥrâm	إحرام	the state of consecration for Hajj or 'umrah; the special clothing worn by the pilgrim in such a state
innâ lillâhi wa innâ ilayhi râji'oon	إنّا لله وإنّا إليه راجعون	'to Allah we belong and to Him is our return'; a phrase uttered during times of difficulty [*Soorat al-Baqarah* (2: 156)]

[1] The Arabic words are transliterated according to the conventions of the Transliteration Chart found in this book. If a word has become part of the English language (i.e. is found in a dictionary of Standard English), that spelling is used in this book and appears first in this Glossary, with the transliterated form in brackets after it.

i'tikâf	إعتكاف	seclusion in the mosque solely for the purpose of worship
khazeerah	خزيرة	a dish prepared by cutting meat into small pieces and covering it with water. When the meat is almost done, some flour is sprinkled on to it (and cooked for a while).
maḥram	محرم	a degree of consanguinity precluding marriage; a man whom a woman may never marry due to the close blood or marriage relationship. e.g., father, brother, son, uncle, and father-in-law
seerah	سيرة	biography
subḥân Allâh	سبحان اللّٰه	glory be to Allah
Sunnah	سنّة	the practice and collected sayings of Prophet Muhammad (ﷺ) that together with the Qur'an forms the basis of Islamic law
tashahhud	التشهُّد	the testimony that states that there is none worthy of worship other than Allah, He has no partners, and that Muhammad (ﷺ) is His Slave and His Messenger
Ummah	أمّة	community or nation: *usu.* used to refer to the entire global community of Muslims